TaKeDoWn

TaKeDoWn

Joyce
Sweeney

Marshall Cavendish
New York
London
Singapore

Marshall Cavendish
99 White Plains Road
Tarrytown, NY 10591
www.marshallcavendish.us

Library of Congress Cataloging-in-Publication Data
Sweeney, Joyce.
Takedown / by Joyce Sweeney.—1st ed.
p. cm.
Summary: A murderer on the run from the authorities crashes thirteen-year-old Joe's pizza party and takes
him and his friends as hostages.
ISBN 0-7614-5175-7
[1. Hostages—Fiction. 2. Friendship—Fiction. 3. Family life—Fiction. 4. Criminals—Fiction.] I. Title.

PZ7.S97427Tak 2004
[Fic]—dc22
2004046475

The text of this book is set in Galliard.
Book design by Anahid Hamparian

Printed in the United States of America
First edition

10 9 8 7 6 5 4 3 2

For my hero, "The Nature Boy" Ric Flair,
who taught me everything I know about survival

When Joe walked in the front door, he could already hear his sister Elizabeth in the kitchen talking to their mother. He threw down his backpack and ran, stopping just outside the doorway to settle down and make a cool entrance. "Hey." He pushed through the saloon-style doors, one of the many bizarre ideas his mom got from Home and Garden TV.

Mrs. Anderson stood at the island, making something the color of putty in the blender. Joe studied her outfit for clues. Jeans, a denim vest—a little too dressy for an evening at home. But the real giveaway was under the vest—a black leotard. This was a writing-class outfit if he'd ever seen one. Joe's heart soared.

As he slid onto a stool next to Elizabeth, however, he couldn't help noticing his sister's Cheshire-cat grin. Conflicting data! Most likely, the final decision hadn't been made.

"What are you making?" he called over the racket. "It smells great!" Actually it smelled like overripe bananas and made him want to vomit, but if he had to drink one of his mother's concoctions to have his Friday Night Fusion party, then so be it.

Mrs. Anderson finally pushed the stop button. The drink churned and frothed like corrosive acid. "It's a recipe from this." She held up her latest diet bible, *The Primate Plan*. The theory of this one was that if we ate a "browser diet," like our monkey ancestors, we'd all be thin and healthy. So bananas and tropical fruits had been showing up at every meal. Joe now examined all his casseroles carefully in case any ants or termites were going to make an appearance. His mother would do anything in her battle against wide hips.

Mrs. Anderson poured her hell-brew into two glasses, so it was obviously an after-school snack for her twin monkeys.

"Oooh, this looks delicious!" Elizabeth purred, stirring her muck with a spoon.

Joe stared into its chalky depths. It smelled like sherbet and the tire-shine stuff they used at the car wash. "Cheers!" Joe raised his glass, clinked with Elizabeth and took three swallows, battling his gag reflex.

Mrs. Anderson was at the sink, with her back to them, so Elizabeth and Joe were free to make disgust-faces at each other as they set down their glasses. Joe mouthed, *Is she going?* but Elizabeth just shrugged, eyes twinkling. Joe mouthed another word to her about her general unhelpfulness. "So, Mom," he said. "What's the verdict?"

Mrs. Anderson turned around, curling a lock of palomino hair around her finger. When the three of them were together, they looked like a shampoo commercial. "I don't know what to do," she said. "I know you guys are old enough to be by yourselves. . . ."

"And then some," Joe encouraged.

"And this writing class is a real opportunity for me. . . ."

"Invitation only," Joe reminded her. "A chance to study with your hero, Emily Whats-Her-Name."

"Lockwood, honey. Emily Lockwood. She won the Windham Prize for Poetry last year."

"Right! And you've got an invitation to be in her class. Come on, Mom. This is the chance of a lifetime!" Joe noticed his knuckles were white as they gripped the serving counter.

"Oh, come off it!" Elizabeth groaned. "Mom, you know he's just playing you! Joe wouldn't read a poem if somebody put a gun to his head! He just wants to have a bunch of his geeky friends over here to watch Fusion, and they don't want you here because they're going to scream and yell and make all those delightful obscene gestures they've learned from their fake heroes!" She adjusted the clip in her hair and offered Joe a dimply smile.

Joe's voice squeaked with outrage. "There's no obscene gestures in wrestling!" He demonstrated a series of gestures for his mother. "This means, 'united forever' and this means 'planetary revolution' and this. . ."

"Joe, what I can't understand is your whole interest in this!" his mother said. "You and your friends are all so intelligent. You're gifted! You read at a twelfth-grade level. . . ."

"You want me to have the guys over to watch Evening at the Pops?"

"No, but this seems like just the opposite of what I'd expect you to like—it's violent, it's fake. . . ."

"It's not supposed to be real, Mom." Joe tried to be patient. "It's like . . . stories. It's modern mythology. Remember that article I showed you?"

"In TV Guide!" Elizabeth put in.

Joe gave her a look and turned back to his mother. "Still. It's about heroes and villains. Values. Like tonight. We're going to find out if the Solar System's plan to destroy Jack Shine worked at the Pay-Per-View last night. If he lost the match, he has to leave wrestling forever. And we know the Solar System was planning to drug him. . . ."

"This must be Daddy's genes coming out," Elizabeth said.

Joe was fed up. "What about you and Buffy the Vampire Slayer, Miss Einstein?"

"Okay! Okay!" Mrs. Anderson held up her hands. "We're all entitled to our own recreations. It's like me reading romance novels, I guess. That's really not the point, Joe. This is about me trusting you to have a bunch of guys over without supervision. . . ."

"When Quentin Charles Dorn is still on the loose," Elizabeth added.

"Okay! Here's the real agenda!" Joe cried. "First of all, unless he's a complete idiot, Quentin Charles Dorn is halfway to Kansas by now. . . ."

"The police think he's still in the area," Elizabeth argued.

"Mom!" Joe whined. "Tell her Quentin Charles Dorn is not going to pick this house, of all the houses in the greater Fort Lauderdale area tonight. . . ."

"We're just all on edge, honey," Mrs. Anderson said. "He's killed two people. He must be clever or the police would have gotten him by now."

"There's been nothing new for four days!" Joe argued. "He's gone! And anyway, name one day of the week when there's not a million other killers in South Florida. You can't wait for an end to crime to leave us alone. We're almost fourteen years old! Steve Hennig has us over all the time when his parents aren't there!"

"I don't care what other parents do. I'm the one responsible for you, Joe."

Joe slapped the counter. "I'm not a little wimp, Mom! And all the guys will be here—Steve and Ramon and Nathan and Tony. . . ."

"Tony Ong?" Mrs. Anderson said.

More complications. "He's fine now. He's been back in school for a month."

Luckily, Elizabeth interrupted. "If he's going to fill up the house with testosterone, I want to have Francesca over."

Joe was about to object automatically, when he realized what Elizabeth had actually said and suddenly shifted gears. "I have no problem with that," he said, struggling to sound neutral as he thought about Francesca. "That's only fair. Come on, Mom. Seven kids. There's strength in numbers."

She had her arms folded. "Not in numbers of kids, Joe. I know what happens when a bunch of kids get together with no adults. Pretty soon you're making crank calls and stopping up the toilet for fun. . . ."

Joe was getting frustrated. "Maybe you did that when

you were our age, but kids are a lot more mature now."

"So what does that mean? Drinking and sex?"

"Mom! Come on! I want to have four guys over. They all drink sodas or juice! I want to order a couple of pizzas, which I can pay for with my own money, and we want to watch a two-hour wrestling show. I promise you, Mom, when that thing's on, nobody moves from in front of the set, not even during commercials! That's all I want and it's not too much to ask . . . for a good son like me. . . ." He made his face sweet and appealing.

"Oh, please!" Elizabeth rolled her eyes.

Mrs. Anderson walked slowly toward the serving counter. She put her hands on top of Joe's, looking directly into his eyes. "Why is this so important to you?"

Joe hesitated. He had his pride, but he'd also learned with a psychologist for a mother, sometimes a little self-exposure could get you right in the door. "Because I'm shorter than all my friends and I have a twin sister who's a girl and I just want to do a guy thing and not be treated like I'm two years old."

Elizabeth, beside him, gave a cynical snort. But Joe could tell from his mother's eyes, he'd scored. She smiled. "Okay, Joe, you win," she said.

Joe could practically hear the bell for the opening match.

✗ ✗ ✗

Still, it wasn't a completely done deal until she went out that door. Joe had learned from experience that his mom could cave on anything at the last minute. Before dinner, she had put her purse and a notebook beside the door, which meant her resolve was weak and she was trying to bolster it. And there was Elizabeth, who was secretly scared to death. She looked like she had given up, but Joe knew better. They could always read each other's minds. Twinsight, Mrs. Anderson called it.

"If something does happen," Elizabeth asked at dinner, "do you want us to beep you first and then call 911 or . . ."

Joe threw his fork down, while Mrs. Anderson froze at the horror of her daughter's question. "You-uh-call 911 first and then beep me." She pushed her plate of nuts and berries back for a second.

Joe knew he had to be aggressive. "Cut it out, Elizabeth! Nothing's going to happen!"

Without even glancing at him, Elizabeth raised her swanlike hand, which was holding the remote. "Let's watch the news," she said.

Joe groaned. They sat through the story of the exotic dancer whose body was found in a cardboard box in a canal, the pedophile who was driving the school bus in Kendall, and then the big enchilada—an update on Quentin Charles Dorn. His handsome young face filled the screen. The four different ways he could look—with and without glasses, with or without facial hair. The police were positive he was still in Broward County, probably in the downtown area.

"Nowhere near Coral Springs!" Joe pointed out.

"If they really knew where he was, they'd get him," Elizabeth said.

Mel Taylor, the reporter from Channel 10, went on,

"If you see anyone who fits this description, police are advising you to call them immediately. Do not approach or attempt to detain him. He is known to be armed and extremely dangerous."

Joe noticed his mother was watching the screen as if hypnotized. Mel Taylor was reviewing the two murders Dorn had committed. It started at Florida Atlantic University, where he'd shot an English professor who was giving him a failing grade. Apparently, without that credit he wasn't going to graduate. There were plenty of witnesses, but he got away and didn't go home. His roommate was questioned over and over, but it was obvious he was on the run. Three days later, he surfaced, shooting a guy on a side street downtown and hijacking his car, which for some reason he drove only four blocks before he ditched it. Because of the carjacking, he was considered to be desperate and dangerous. Mel Taylor's report closed with the now-familiar quote from John Riley of the Broward sheriff's office, "This guy will kill you for a sandwich."

"Mom, please, turn it off," Joe said. "Elizabeth is getting herself all worked up for nothing."

Miraculously, Mrs. Anderson turned to Elizabeth and said, "He's right. Turn it off."

Moving at superslow speed, Elizabeth clicked the remote and the close-up of Quentin Charles Dorn's face vanished.

"Elizabeth, I want to say something to you." Mrs. Anderson nibbled on an almond. "All day long, I've been looking for excuses not to take this class. I'm not good enough. I don't have time to write. And this big one—it isn't safe to leave you guys alone. I've been doing that all my life, guys. That's why I'm a guidance counselor when I really wanted to be a poet. That's why I married the first guy who asked me, even when I knew it was a mistake. I don't mean to put myself down, but I think I've been way too timid all my life. And what kind of role model is that for you? Especially you, Elizabeth. Look how nervous you are about doing something different. Have I done that to you?"

Thank you, God, Joe thought. Feminism is kicking in. There was no stronger force in this household.

"You and I are enabling each other, Elizabeth. I'm keeping you a baby and you're keeping me from growing as a person. We both need to be more like Joe. He's excited about a challenge."

Yes! Feminism and psychobabble! "You have to go, Mom," Joe said, carefully avoiding Elizabeth's gaze. "You have to do this."

Mrs. Anderson smiled. "You're right. I'm going right now before I change my mind. Will you guys do the dishes?"

"Sure." Joe was already stacking plates.

"Okay." She rose uncertainly. "The class is from seven to nine."

"Well, the show is from eight to ten," Joe said. "Can't you go for coffee with somebody afterward?"

She laughed. "Don't push it, sweetie." Mrs. Anderson grabbed her stuff. "I'm going before I lose my nerve." She came over and quickly kissed each of them on top of the head. "Lock the door after me."

"Okay," said Joe. *Go. Go.*

"All right." The door closed. Both of them stood still, listening to the car rev up. Neither moved until the last sound of the engine died away.

Joe was surprised at how nervous he suddenly was. "We'll have a blast tonight, Elizabeth," he said. "You'll see." He went to the front door and flipped the bolt so hard it sounded like gunshot.

The living room was dark, except for the frantic flicker of the TV. Pyrotechnic sparks showered the set of Friday Night Fusion, like a thousand bottles of champagne exploding at once. The sellout crowd at the MGM Grand in Las Vegas roared and waved banners. Announcers Billy MacRae and Mike "The Maniac" Mulligan were at ringside, throwing out teasers about the stunning, world-shaking events that had taken place at last night's Pay-Per-View, *Joker's Wild*. "The world of professional wrestling is changed forever," the Maniac declared.

Joe handed out bags of chips and snacks to the guys sprawled on the floor. Steve Hennig—a big blond guy who looked like a future wrestler himself—and Ramon Guerrero—who was compared to Antonio Banderas by all the girls in their class—were whistling at the screen, making gestures of support for their favorite alliance of wrestlers, the powerful Solar System. Nathan Jericho, Joe's best friend, sat a little apart from them, and reached up to help Joe hand out the bags of snacks.

Tony Ong sat on the fringe, ominously silent. Joe didn't think he had spoken at all since he came in the door. It had been a toss-up whether or not to invite him. He'd always been part of the group, so it would have been mean to exclude him just because he had to take a "leave of absence" from school. Still, Joe worried about Tony bringing the party down. At his best, Tony was silent, moody . . . distracted. It was like he was partially focused on some other world. For example, he was hunched over now, not watching the screen, staring at his hands like some frail old guy on a park bench. Joe decided to keep a careful eye on him tonight.

Steve tugged open his bag of Cheez Doodles, and they exploded out the top like little trick snakes. "You're gonna have a bad night, Joe. It sounds like your boy went down at the Pay-Per-View."

"We'll see." Joe couldn't focus on that yet. He was still playing host. He took the remaining bags—pretzels and some kind of air-puffed stuff his mom thought was healthy—to the couch at the back of the living room, where the girls sat together. Elizabeth looked bored, but Francesca Hart was leaning forward, like she might get into it. Joe was already considering marrying Francesca sometime in the future. If she turned out to be a wrestling fan, that would settle it. She didn't know Joe liked her, of course, since she was Elizabeth's best friend. Plus, she was African American and Joe didn't know if she even looked at white boys that way. Joe thought of himself as a complete geek with girls, unlike Steve or Ramon, who both had girlfriends. But Joe could look at Francesca free of charge: her tilted brown eyes, her soft, springy hair, her child-smile, her amazing fashion statements. Tonight she wore lime green jeans and a matching linen shirt, a blue-and-green butterfly clip in her hair. She was a gymnast, a straight-A student, a clarinet player. Even her posture was perfect. Joe didn't think he had ever seen her scratch herself or sneeze in public or any human thing like that. In his mind he called her "The Goddess."

She added luster to a night that was already Joe's dream come true. He activated the portable phone, feeling powerful. "Delivery order? Shut up you guys! Yes, that's the address. One meat-fanatic, one garden-special and one with pepperoni and extra cheese."

"Sauce!" Nathan prompted.

"And some extra sauce on the side. Anything else you guys?"

"Bread," said Steve. "Hang up, man. They just said Jack Shine is coming out to make an announcement."

"Large twisty-bread. Thanks!" Joe hung up fast. "He's coming out right now?"

"Coming out to say good-bye!" Steve taunted. "Probably on a stretcher!" He slammed a big fist into his big palm.

"In your dreams!" Joe shot back. "Your planetary punks are going to jail—that's what's gonna happen! I hope Shine presses charges!"

"Shhh!" Nathan hissed. "Here he comes!"

The living room hushed, as did the arena in Las Vegas. Then there was the sound of a clock ticking, louder and louder. The Jumbo-tron showed videos of clock hands spinning out of control as Jack Shine, "The Human Time Bomb," parted the curtains and stood at the end of the aisle. He wore his trademark robe, twinkling with eternity lights. More pyrotechnics showered down as he began to walk to the ring.

Nathan and Joe raised their arms over their heads and tapped their wrists, mimicking the "time's up" gesture Shine always performed before he finished his opponents off with his Moment of Truth sleeper hold.

Steve and Ramon, along with about half the crowd in Vegas, booed and catcalled. Jack Shine had gone back and forth from good to bad so many times, the fans were split on whether or not they liked him.

Steve began to rock from side to side, cupping his hands to his mouth, as if he could project his voice all the way to Nevada. "Looo-ser, looo-ser!"

"Go to a nursing home, man!" Ramon snarled at the screen. "You are so finished!"

"Twenty-seven-time world heavyweight champion!" Joe cried in Shine's defense.

Elizabeth jumped in. "Only because the scriptwriters keep taking it away from him and giving it back!"

"Bor-ring!" chanted Ramon.

"That's a lame outfit," Francesca volunteered.

Joe winced. He wanted Francesca to like Jack Shine. Pushing fifty, Shine was definitely part of the "old" world of wrestling. One of the few left with a real wrestling background. He'd been a talented amateur in college and had even been on the US Olympic team in the eighties, before he turned "pro." When he was a good guy, they stressed his commitment to excellence and tradition. When he was bad, he was a grasping, power-mad, ruthless cheat.

None of this mattered to Joe. His interest in Shine was simple. At six feet and weighing only 240, Shine was tiny for a wrestler, but, thanks to the scriptwriters, he regularly beat up guys twice his size. For two hours a week, Joe liked being in a world where that could happen, real or not.

Shine stepped through the ropes and spoke into a microphone he'd picked up somewhere at ringside. Everyone hushed. "Las Vegas, Nevada!" he cried, bugging out his eyes and flipping back his long, platinum hair. "My favorite town!"

The crowd went wild, waving their banners.

"He says that every week no matter where he is!" Elizabeth said.

"I've got a message for my friends in the Solar System," Shine said as the camera pulled in close to his face. "Your little plan didn't work!"

"Bor-ring!" said Ramon. "Bring out some wrestlers and get rid of this guy."

"Mercury?" Shine went on. "I know you're hiding back in the dressing room somewhere, shaking in your little silver boots. You thought you could give me a cup of coffee backstage last night and I would drink it? You must think I'm as stupid as you!"

"Yeah!" Joe hollered.

"I not only didn't drink it, I took it to a lab and had it analyzed."

"All right!" Joe screamed as the Vegas fans roared. "Mercury's going down!"

"Rat poison!" Shine declared. "It was laced with rat poison!"

"Oh, man!" said Steve.

"So here's the deal, pal. We can do it two ways. Either you wrestle me tonight and give me the satisfaction of kicking your tail all around this ring, or I can show those lab results and the videotape of you handing me the coffee to the police and you can trade in your mylar suit for prison gray!"

Nathan and Joe hooted with joy and slapped hands.

"And if I win tonight, the Solar System has to break up . . . forever!"

"No!" Steve screamed. "No!"

"How can you guys even pretend to believe?" Elizabeth began.

"Quiet!" Joe yelled. "He's almost done."

Another extreme close-up. "Every man has a moment of truth," Shine chanted with quiet, controlled rage.

"When he is tested for all he's worth," Nathan and Joe chanted along. "And Mercury . . . YOUR TIME IS UP!"

Shine threw the microphone down and stalked off as the crowd roared. Joe fell back, exhausted and thrilled. He'd love to see the Solar System broken up. They were always trying to make Jack Shine look bad.

"The Solar System will gang up on him," Ramon said.

"That flabby old geek doesn't stand a chance."

"Do they ever wrestle?" Francesca asked. "Or do they just talk?"

"They'll wrestle!" Steve said. "Maybe tonight the Solar System will finally put that moron out of business."

A commercial came on. "What do you guys want to drink?" Joe asked.

"Beer!" Steve called.

Joe laughed. "Second choice."

"Coke!"

Everyone else called out orders.

"I'll help you." Francesca slid off the couch and disappeared into the shadows.

Could this night get any better? Joe followed her down the hallway to the kitchen.

A pie-shaped wedge of light from the open refrigerator cast a glow on Francesca's face and sparkled in her hair. Joe had to remind himself to breathe. "It's four Cokes, one cranberry, one apple, and a ginger ale for me," he said.

"Elizabeth told me you like me." Her tone was flat. Not angry exactly, but definitely accusing.

"Huh?" *How could Elizabeth do this to me?*

"She said you like me." She half turned toward Joe, still holding the door. Her face was half light and half shadow.

"Sure I like you," Joe said carefully. "You're a nice person."

She shifted her weight. "Not like that. Like a boy likes a girl."

Was she mad? Was it an outrage that a geek like him dared to look at her?

"Hey! Quit spacing out! I asked you a question!"

Yes, ma'am! "Uh, I don't know how to answer you."

The refrigerator made a complaining sound as she continued to hold the door open. "Just tell me the truth."

The noise from the living room had escalated again. The commercial must be over. Joe pictured himself there on the floor, safe with his buddies. He decided to try faking his own hostility. "Okay! I happen to think you're really pretty! Is there a law against that?"

"Thank you! You should have told me instead of Elizabeth!"

"Well, now you know!" Why were they fighting?

She closed the door and vanished into semidarkness. "So what do you want to do about it?"

Do about it? Joe took a step back, bumping into the stove. "I don't want to do anything about it. It's just how I feel." Then, he took a step closer. "What would we do about it?"

In the darkness, she was all voice, powerful. "I'll tell you something, Joe. I liked you since last year."

Joe's whole idea of the universe shifted. He'd always known bad stuff could sneak up on you when you weren't looking, but good stuff? This was new. "Yeah?"

"Yeah. But I don't know how I feel about going out with a white boy."

Joe was impressed with her honesty. With a person this direct, you could say anything, never be afraid to speak.

She must have taken his silence for criticism. "That's not being racist, Joe. I just don't know if I want to freak out my parents, you know?"

"Sure, yeah. I know. I understand."

"What's going on out there?" Steve's voice boomed from the living room, followed by peals of laughter.

"We better get back," Joe said. "They're making up stories."

"Wait."

Joe waited.

"I was thinking maybe we could secretly be boyfriend and girlfriend," she said. "If we don't tell anybody."

"What would that mean?" Joe's voice cracked a little.

"We would just know it. Write me a note on Monday and put it in my locker. And then I'll write a note back to you."

Joe wondered how many drafts he'd have to write before he figured out what was an acceptable note. "Okay."

She smiled her pretty curving smile. "Want to seal it with a kiss?"

A rush of hot feelings closed in on Joe so fast he couldn't speak. Then somebody tapped his shoulder and he screamed like he'd been shot.

"Sorry, buddy." Nathan flipped on the overhead light, blinding Joe. "I'm the search party. Everybody thought you guys got lost." He gave Joe a wicked grin. "I think the problem is, you were trying to find the refrigerator in the dark. There it is!" He pointed.

Joe turned away from him, brushed awkwardly past Francesca and began loading soda cans into his arms. "What did I miss?"

"The Bad Dog just took the cruiserweight belt away from Freddie Sanchez. Ramon is in there grieving. Shine and Mercury are coming up next. What did I miss?"

Francesca reached in and got a bottle of cranberry juice, brushing lightly against Joe. She straightened up and walked past Nathan, gesturing him aside. "Nothing you would have understood." She walked out of the kitchen. Both boys stared after her.

Nathan slowly walked over and helped Joe with the sodas. "Wow! Is something going on?"

Was a secret a secret from your best friend? "I don't know."

"You don't know?" Nathan began, but Joe walked out on him, feeling guilty.

The match between Mercury and Shine was already underway. Joe passed out drinks, watching the screen all the time. Mercury's friends, the other planets, were all at ringside, distracting the referee, sneaking punches at Shine if he got too close to them, trying to throw foreign objects in for Mercury to use. Jack Shine was a loner and therefore at a disadvantage.

"He could drop the title belt right here tonight!" Steve cried.

"If that was going to happen, it would have happened at the Pay-Per-View," said Nathan, as he gave Joe a Big Look. Joe tried to think how he could apologize without betraying his secret with Francesca. It seemed impossible.

"Bor-ring!" Ramon chanted. He wore his hair very long with a headband. Rage over the last match still showed on his face.

"He'll think of something," Joe said. "He always does."

But Shine was on the ropes, literally. Pounded and

pummeled, his platinum hair hung in sweaty strings. Venus was distracting the referee by pretending to bend over and pick something up off the floor. This gave Pluto the opportunity to grab Jack Shine's arms through the ropes and hold him helpless while Mercury repeatedly kicked him. Neptune was about to throw a folding chair into the ring.

Suddenly Shine seemed to get a second wind. This often happened to him in low spots. He would get a burst of energy out of nowhere and make a surprise comeback.

"Here he goes, watch him now!" Nathan called.

Shine shook off Pluto with ease, and then did his characteristic dance in the middle of the ring, to show the fans he felt fine. He raised his arms over his head and tapped his wrist.

"Time's up!" Joe and Nathan screamed in unison— along with half the crowd in Las Vegas.

Shine reached under his knee pad and extracted what looked like a small iron bar. He closed it into his fist and swung at Mercury. Mercury staggered and fell. Shine put the iron bar in his tights. At that moment, the referee finally turned around in time to see Shine cover Mercury for the pinfall.

Nathan and Joe counted together. "One! Two! Three!" The bell clanged. The referee held up Jack Shine's hand. The crowd in Vegas went wild.

"Bor-ring!" said Ramon. "That old geek must have stock in the company."

"He cheated!" Elizabeth cried.

"He had to!" Joe said. He looked at Nathan, expecting a

victory hand slap, but Nathan looked the other way. *Great.*

"Does the Solar System really have to break up?" Steve sounded like he was going to cry. The doorbell rang. "There's the pizza!" he added, sounding considerably consoled.

Joe fished in his pocket for the huge wad of cash he'd saved up for the past few weeks by mowing lawns and washing the neighbors' cars. He went to the door.

"Hi." The pizza guy glanced past Joe into the room. Something about that glance was wrong, made Joe look into the guy's face as he tore open the Velcro on the pizza pouch. So Joe knew it was Quentin Charles Dorn even before he drew out the handgun, aimed it at Joe's face, and said, "Step back, kid."

The amazing thing was, no one screamed. As Joe slowly backed away from the door, he didn't even hear a gasp, or see a flinch in his peripheral vision. Maybe this was what they called shock.

Dorn, though, was pretty animated. In the dark room, his eyes looked huge—some kind of pale, lunar color. His movements were jerky, like he wasn't sure what to do first. Still aiming at Joe, he bent his knees and gently placed the pizza warmer on the floor.

Then he straightened up, reached around awkwardly behind him, and made several grabs at the door handle, before he could get it shut. Now, he was swiveling his head, looking at the kids on either side of him. "Who else is in this house?" he shouted. His voice was startling. He sounded like an ordinary young guy. Somehow Joe had expected some kind of supernatural growl.

"Just us, just the seven of us," Joe said quickly.

Dorn stared at him. He was handsome, clean-cut except

for a couple days' growth of beard. "You better not be lying," he said. "Why is it so dark in here? You. Go over to that lamp and turn it on, very slowly."

Joe managed to stumble toward the couch where the girls were sitting and turn on the floor lamp. His back was to the girls, but he could now clearly see the faces of the guys sitting on the floor. He hoped his own face didn't look that scared.

Dorn glanced at the windows. Joe figured he was making sure the drapes were shut. "And shut off that TV, too. It's driving me nuts!"

Why me? Joe wondered, since Dorn was still talking exclusively to him. He took the long walk back to the table where the remote was, careful to keep his motions slow and non-threatening. The gun barrel followed him.

A commercial was on for a new video game where you killed people and collected their souls. Joe pushed the power button. The screen flashed into darkness and silence. Suddenly, the whole room seemed more tense.

This is real.

"Okay, good." Dorn nodded at Joe. "Good." He gestured with the gun, past Joe and toward the back door and the kitchen behind him. "Where's the door to the garage? Is it that one?"

Please talk to someone else for a while so I can pass out or wet myself or something.

"Yes."

Dorn's expression relaxed. He looked a lot like a camp

counselor Joe had had once. Nothing like a guy who would "kill you for a sandwich."

"You're doing great, kid. Where's the keys to the car?"

Something flipped over in Joe's rib cage. "My mom has the car. There's no car."

Dorn's chest rose and fell. His face flushed, as if he were embarrassed. "Oh, God," he said softly. He started to run his free hand through his hair, but his fingers bumped the pizza delivery cap. He tore it off and skimmed it into the room like a Frisbee. "Why am I still wearing this stupid HAT?" he screamed.

One of the boys, probably Tony Ong, let out a low whine, like a caged dog.

Dorn took another deep breath and spoke to Joe in a tight voice. "When does she get back?"

Joe croaked, "Not till after ten."

Dorn exploded with a string of curses that made everyone flinch as if his words were little rocks flying in every direction. "I went through all this for a house with no car?" he cried. "Wouldn't you figure a house getting a pizza delivery has the car in the garage?" He seemed to be pleading with them, as if their verdict on his judgment was important.

Joe, however, was focused on the phrase, "I went through all this."

"Did you shoot the pizza guy?" he blurted before he realized that was a bad, bad question to ask.

But Dorn was lost in his deliberations. "I sure as hell

can't drive out of here in that pizza truck with the big slice on the roof," he muttered. "Anyway, they probably have some kind of clock on those guys, right?"

Joe wondered if they were supposed to volunteer ideas for the guy. He was startled to hear Nathan speak up. "We don't have what you want, so you better get moving before one of the neighbors calls 911 about whatever you did in the driveway."

Dorn turned and stared at him, as if the furniture had spoken. "What did you say?"

Tony pulled his knees up and buried his face in them. Ramon and Steve were staring at Dorn like two scared kids about to be whacked by the principal. Joe was surprised that the jocks seemed to be shutting down, while he and Nathan were at least functional. Nathan's face was the calmest, but tremors were running through him so hard his hair was shaking. "I wasn't telling you what to do," he said carefully. "That was just how it looked to me."

Dorn stared at him a second longer, then lowered the gun an inch or two. "That's how it looks to me, too." He turned back to Joe. "This is your house, right?"

"Yes." Joe saw no point in mentioning Elizabeth's status. *Why volunteer anything you didn't have to?*

Dorn ran his free hand over his face. "Is there any money around here?"

Joe dug in his pocket and got out the two twenties and the ten he had for pizza money. "You can have this."

Dorn barked a laugh. "Yeah, I know I can have it."

He stepped forward and snatched the money, like he thought Joe was going to pull a kickboxing maneuver, and Joe realized this guy was really afraid. "What about the rest of you? Empty your pockets, take off all your jewelry. Move! I don't have that much time."

Everybody complied, but the pickings were slim. The only good things were Steve's cell phone and Tony's watch. The cash, besides Joe's, looked like less than twenty dollars. Dorn seemed especially annoyed with the girls, whose jewelry was all plastic and enamel. Dorn looked at Tony's watch before stuffing it in his pocket. "How about the rest of the house? Your mom have jewelry? You have a dad?"

Joe laughed involuntarily. "My dad lives in Michigan," he said. "My mom isn't big on jewelry."

Dorn's eyes narrowed. "Let's make sure. Show me where she keeps it. You girls . . ." He waved the gun at Francesca and Elizabeth. "Come here and sit with the guys. I want you all sitting in a nice, terrified huddle while he shows me around." Elizabeth jumped up and scurried across the room. Francesca walked slowly, just this side of defiant. Dorn's eyes followed the sway of her hips as she walked. *Don't get upset*, Joe thought.

Dorn brandished the gun at the group on the floor. "If I hear any noise I don't like coming from this room"—he beckoned Joe forward—"your little buddy here—what's your name, kid?"

"Joe." It was hard to walk, talk, and shake all at the

same time. As soon as he got close to Dorn, Joe was pulled forward, into a sort of gentle headlock by Dorn's left arm. The guy hadn't showered in a long time, either.

"Any noises at all, any movements and there'll be pieces of Joe's brain all over the place—okay?" Dorn illustrated his point by pressing the gun barrel to the crown of Joe's head. Joe's stomach churned. The gun barrel was *warm.*

Dorn stepped backward into the hall, dragging Joe with him. "Mom's bedroom is back here?"

"Yes." Joe could hardly breathe.

Then Elizabeth did something stupid. She tapped her heart with her right hand. It was a signal that went all the way back to nursery school, used mostly for grief at parting, but also to show support if the other twin was in trouble. Joe hadn't seen it in years. Dorn let go of Joe, who fell on his ass in the doorway between the living room and hall.

Meanwhile Dorn had lunged forward and aimed the gun right at Elizabeth's forehead. "Did you give him a *signal?*" His voice arced up in the soprano range. "You think you're a little bunch of commandos, don't you? What did that mean? Tell me and don't lie!"

Elizabeth's face contorted and her words pushed out in a sob. "It just means I love him! He's my brother! I wasn't giving him any"—she paused and choked, then recovered—"signal."

It had flitted through Joe's mind that he could jump on Dorn's back, but he realized that kind of thing would only work in the movies. Instead, he got up slowly and began to plead. "We're twins, Mr. Dorn! She probably didn't even know she was doing it. We make signs like that all the time. Please, please stop pointing that gun at her. She didn't mean anything!"

Elizabeth lost it completely. Francesca wrapped her arms around her from behind, like a cocoon.

Dorn seemed to be shifting gears. He straightened up slowly, taking several deep breaths.

"Don't you want to get the jewelry and get going?" Joe continued in the same begging tone. He hoped he wasn't about to cry.

Dorn backed up from the kids on the floor, who were now making a terrified huddle, just as he'd described. "That was stupid," he scolded Elizabeth. "I could have killed you. Don't do stupid things like that any more." He backed up till he was even with Joe. "And you don't tell me what to do!" he said.

"Okay." Sweat broke out over Joe's whole body. Dorn gave him a shove down the hallway. "Show me where her room is." He pointed the gun at the living room one more time. "You little morons don't move a muscle!"

Joe could hardly think straight. The thing with Elizabeth had left him rattled and now he had to show this creep his mother's bedroom. Joe struggled to remember what was important. The guy knew he had to leave fairly fast. They all needed to just stay calm and give him what he wanted and they'd make it. Joe tried not to think about the

TV shows he'd seen where people were killed just because they were witnesses. That was just TV. Wasn't it?

"This is her room," he said, fumbling with the light switch.

The bed wasn't made. His mother's basketball jersey, the one she slept in, was on the floor. Her big stuffed gorilla sat in a rocking chair by the window. On her dresser was a collection of oddball things made for her by the kids she counseled; a Mr. Potato Head, a little box made of Popsicle sticks, a sculpture of a hand sticking up like *Night of the Living Dead*. On the far wall was her favorite poster: Norman Bates eating a sandwich under a big stuffed owl. The caption read, WE ALL GO A LITTLE MAD SOMETIMES. Joe watched Dorn taking all this in and felt embarrassed. Then he realized how ridiculous it was to be embarrassed in front of a guy who might blow them all away. Did it really matter at the moment if Dorn thought Joe's mom was a geek? Then he realized it wasn't shame that was making his face burn. It was anger that this creep was getting to look at their private stuff this way.

Dorn had located Mrs. Anderson's jewelry box and yanked it open. The hinge made a popping sound. He pawed through the rubble, angrily tossing out Mother's Day gifts from Elizabeth and Joe like they were crap. "Boy, you weren't kidding, Joe." He held up a string of pink crystal beads she'd worn last Halloween with her flapper costume. "This stuff sucks! Are you sure she hasn't got the good stuff in a strong box somewhere?"

Joe broke off his fantasy of wrapping the beads around Dorn's neck and slowly squeezing. "She's not a jewelry person."

"I'll say." Dorn slammed the lid, having palmed Mrs. Anderson's wedding ring and her gold locket from Grandma. He glanced around the room again. "Looks like a dyke's room."

Joe's mouth opened automatically, but he managed to choke off whatever it was his stomach wanted to say. *Just stay alive and get him out of here.*

Dorn put the headlock back on. "Come on, I gotta get going." He hurried Joe down the hall, back to the other guys who looked like they, indeed, hadn't moved a muscle. Elizabeth's eyes were red and Tony still had his head down. The smell of pizza had filled the whole room.

Dorn seemed to be at a loss. He looked at the front door. "Show me how to get out through the garage."

Joe started to move in that direction, but Dorn was still looking at the kids on the floor. "I need to do something so you little commandos don't call 911 before I can get out of here. . . ."

Again, it was Nathan who spoke up. "We won't. We promise."

"Oh, that's worth a lot." Dorn paused, tapping the gun against his thigh. "I definitely don't want to shoot seven kids. I guess I could tie you up with tape or something. Or lock you in a closet—Joe, is there a closet that locks from the outside?"

Before Joe could answer, Nathan spoke up again. "Why don't you cut all the phone wires?"

Dorn smiled. "That's a good idea. Joe, show me where all the phones are."

Joe felt an overwhelming weariness. It was like this would never be over. Dorn dragged him into the kitchen. "Knife," Dorn commanded. "Just point to where they are."

Joe pointed listlessly to the knife drawer. Dorn selected a steak knife and sliced through the kitchen phone wire. Since he had to do it one-handed, it was a brutal cut that jerked the phone partly out of the wall. Joe was horrified to hear a whimper coming out of his own mouth. Dorn got a big smile on his face. "Did that scare you?" he asked. The tone of his voice was weird, intimate, like kids telling secrets at camp.

This isn't good. I'm coming apart. "There're extensions in all the bedrooms, too." *Please, please get out of here before I start screaming.*

In Elizabeth's room Dorn cut all the computer cables as well as the phone. In Joe's room Dorn paused for a minute, staring at the poster of Jack Shine. Everything in the room was looking wobbly to Joe, like when you try to hold binoculars and look at the stars.

"What's this fruity thing?" Dorn wanted to know.

"He's a wrestler," Joe's voice was low and tired.

"A wrestler! He's wearing a girl's bathrobe, Joe. This can't be good."

"They all wear costumes. It's part of the act. He started

out a long time ago, when they wore a lot of spangles and feathers. . . ." Joe wobbled on his feet and grabbed the wall.

His sudden movement made Dorn lift the gun sharply, but he put it down right away.

"Sit on the floor for a second, Joe, you look like you're gonna pass out," he muttered. He slashed Joe's phone cord and left Joe alone while he ran and slashed the phone in Mrs. Anderson's room. Joe knew he should have taken advantage of that moment but he didn't do a thing. Something in his brain seemed to have stopped working. Dorn came back, took hold of Joe's collar, and gently pulled him up to his feet. "You okay?" he asked, but didn't wait for an answer.

When they got back to the living room, Joe was thinking clearly again. "That's all of them," he said for the benefit of everyone. All the kids knew there was one more phone, the cordless phone Joe had used to order the pizzas. The base was hidden inside the entertainment center. Joe himself couldn't see where he'd put the handset down. With any luck, it was shoved into a chair cushion, or under somebody's jacket or something. Maybe he'd even remembered to put it away.

"It's been fun, kids," Dorn said, moving toward the kitchen. "I wouldn't suggest you run to the neighbors either, because you never know, I might still be around, aiming at you like a sniper." He chuckled to himself. "You should just turn your fruity wrestling show back on and knock yourselves out." He seemed to be staring out the kitchen window. "Is somebody having a party tonight, Joe?"

"What?" Joe said. "I don't know. Just me."

"There's so many cars parked on that street back there . . . . It's gonna make it hard for me to—oh, well . . ." He opened the back door. Joe felt every muscle in his body start to relax, like a cage being opened.

The portable phone rang.

Joe froze. Nathan made some kind of urgent eye contact with him. Dorn gently closed the door and came back into the living room. "Did you lie to me, Joe?" He spoke in a gentle, intimate voice that was much scarier than his growl.

"I forgot the cordless!" Joe cried. "That's all." He looked around frantically for the source of the ringing. It sounded muted. There was almost a hiss at the end of the ring.

"I don't know where I put it down!" Joe said, irrationally afraid if he didn't find the phone fast enough, Dorn would shoot him out of impatience.

The phone rang again. It was nearby. Again, there was a weird, rattling hiss.

Dorn was one step ahead of Joe. He walked over and aimed his gun at Nathan, Steve and Ramon. "Where is it? Where'd you hide it?"

Nathan held up one hand in surrender. With the other, he fished in his bag of Smoky Red Barbecue chips and pulled out the phone, still jangling, and shedding red dust all over the rug.

Dorn jerked the phone out of Nathan's hand, holding

the gun right on Nathan's face while he passed the phone to Joe. "Tell Mom everything's all right," he said.

Joe was shaking so badly, he had to take the phone with both hands. Dorn kept staring at Nathan like he might just shoot him to teach him a lesson. "Hello?" Joe squeaked.

"Hi. Who's this? Is this Joe Anderson?" It was a man with a deep, bass voice.

Joe's training took over, even in this absurd situation. "Yes. Who is this?" he countered. Then he wondered what he was doing. The stranger—danger was already here. This guy might be able to help them.

"I'm Solomon Page with the FBI. Act like you know me, Joe."

"Oh, hi!" Joe said weakly.

"Answer my questions as long as you can without putting yourself in danger. Quentin Dorn is in there with you, right?"

"Yeah."

"How many people are in there?"

"Yeah. The party's great. It's too bad you couldn't come. All the guys are here. All seven of us."

Dorn frowned and tilted his head.

"Is everybody okay?" Page asked.

"Sure. Listen, I gotta go. I think the show is coming back on. . . ."

"Are you in the living room? Is everybody there?"

"Yeah."

Dorn was peering at Joe suspiciously. To his horror, Joe felt himself blush.

Dorn grabbed the phone. "Who the hell are you talking to?" he whispered fiercely, covering the receiver with his hand. "What's going on?"

Joe felt that weak sensation coming back. "It's for you," he said.

Joe noticed that Dorn's hand shook as he held
the phone. "Hello?" For several seconds Dorn's eyes went
blank. He was either listening very intently or zoning out
completely. Joe, who was feeling faint again, stumbled
toward the other kids. Hands reached up to comfort him as
he sat down. He felt exhausted, like he'd been running
laps. Weird pictures of the last half hour flashed in his
mind—the first moment he'd seen the gun as Dorn forced
his way into the house, Dorn grabbing him and shoving
him down the hall, Dorn pawing through his mother's jewelry box, the feel of the warm gun barrel against the top of
his head. Against the top of his head. He touched the part
in his hair gently.

Ramon crossed himself, bowed his head, and closed his
eyes. Joe was surprised that he would do this in front of the
other kids, but he kind of admired it. He wasn't sure how
he felt about the whole God thing. His parents had made
him and Elizabeth go to church and confession until they
were ten, but around the house Catholicism seemed to

be more like a club they belonged to than something to be believed in. His father, especially when he was planning to "go out with the boys," would say things like, "I'm going to hell for sure," but he said it with a big grin on his face. Joe's mother spelled her feelings out more clearly. Everything in the Bible was "cultural mythology," and the Pope was a "tool for reinforcing the patriarchy." But she firmly believed children should have a religious education. Joe had asked her once if she thought it made any sense to pray. She said, with a very guarded expression, that it was probably a good way to clarify things in your mind.

Joe hadn't been interested in clarifying his mind. He had wanted some big, powerful force to come in and give him what he wanted, which at that time, was to stop his parents from divorcing. But he never said the prayer. It felt too silly. Ever since, he had wondered if things could have been different.

He wondered now as he lowered his head and casually folded his hands. *He didn't quite have the nerve for a full sign of the cross.* God? he said tentatively in his mind, feeling like he was some jerk in a chat room, hoping somebody would speak to him.

"You okay?" Nathan whispered.

Joe jumped. "Never better," he mumbled. His face felt like a furnace.

Nathan pointed with his chin to Tony, who still had his face buried in his knees. He was so still, he looked dead. None of them really knew the details of what had happened four months ago.

x x x

They were all in the same gifted program and had most of their classes together. But phys-ed was different. They mixed with the real world there. It was a smooth transition for Steve, who was on the freshman football, baseball, and, of course, wrestling teams. Ramon was a gymnast and a runner. Nathan was okay at sports and excelled at anything that required endurance and willpower, like long-distance running or floor exercise. Joe, being little, struggled with most sports and positively sucked at basketball, where he couldn't even see the basket through the forest of arms and legs. He was surprisingly good at sprinting, though, which made him a good enough base stealer to make the freshman baseball team, so he never felt like a complete loser.

Tony was a complete loser: ran like an old lady, ducked if a ball came toward him, got nauseous after two or three push-ups. The gym teacher, Mr. Flack, hated Tony. He teased, insulted, and called attention to Tony, who then had an even harder time because he was always blushing and trembling. It was painful to watch.

One day, they were rope climbing, which Joe thought he wouldn't be able to do but which turned out to be easy for him. Tony wasn't so lucky. He hung about two feet off the ground like a baby monkey clinging to its mom, apparently unable to move, while all the jocks stood around watching and smirking. Mr. Flack made a disgusted noise and told Tony he'd had it with him, he was wasting everyone's time, and he had to come back after school. They'd stay there, Mr. Flack said, for as long as it took Tony to climb that rope.

In the locker room, Steve, Ramon, Nathan, and Joe clustered around him, offering support and pointers. Tony waved them off and remained in a state of silence for the rest of the day. Joe remembered seeing him in the hall, after school, trudging toward the gym with his bag over his shoulder, like a condemned man walking to the gallows.

The next day, Tony and Mr. Flack were both absent and the rumors were flying. The guidance counselor, Mrs. Rhodes, stepped in and told the gifteds that Mr. Flack had "put too much pressure" on Tony. Tony was a sensitive boy, she said, and "after a rest" he'd be back and "ready to face new challenges." Joe had immediately turned in his seat to make eye contact with Nathan, who nodded grimly and wrapped his arms around his torso in a perfect imitation of a straitjacket. None of them thought they'd ever see Tony again.

For his part, Mr. Flack came back after a week and started saying, "Way to go!" and "Good for you!" to everybody, whether he liked them or not.

Then a month ago Tony reappeared. He was subdued, but seemed okay—like if you said something funny, he'd laugh. The only really different thing was that he walked with his head down, like an old man with osteoporosis. His eyes were perpetually trained on the ground. He had some kind of permanent excuse not to take PE.

X X X

Joe thought about giving Tony a reassuring pat or something, but what if he started barking like a dog? And what
if that would set Dorn off and make him feel like emptying
a few rounds into the source of the noise? Better to leave
Tony in his coma and hope he stayed there.

Being on the phone with the FBI apparently made
Dorn feel like a big shot. He was sprawled on the couch
now, with his big tennis shoes propped up on the coffee
table. "Yeah?" he said. "Well, I don't happen to think
that's true. I'm a huge optimist."

Something made him laugh, or he forced one. "You guys
know I have seven kids in here? Seven? By my calculations,
you have six sets of parents telling you not to screw this up,
right?"

Another laugh. "I know, but the way I look at it, if you
annoy me, all I have to do is plug one of them and toss them
out the door, and then it looks like you guys can't do your
job." He paused, listening again. "Oh, really? Well, bring
them on in, anytime you want to. We'll see what happens."
He took his feet off the coffee table and sat up straight. "I
think so, too, Solomon. I think that's totally possible. I
don't know. I want some time to think about it. You
know?" He gave a laugh that in any other context would
have sounded charming. "I've never been a hostage taker
before and I need to think some things through." Pause.
"That's good, that's really good. I knew we could work

together. . . . No, because I don't want you pressuring me. I hate deadlines. I'll call you. Give me your number. . . . Wait a second." He looked up.

"Joe?" He pantomimed writing on his hand.

Amazed, Joe got up and went to the kitchen for a pad and pen.

"You write for me, Joe," Dorn said. "Okay. 555-3263. Got it?" Into the phone he said, "Joe's been a great little helper. You can tell his mom that. His sister's kind of a pain in the ass, though. . . . No, I told you, I don't know when. Don't make me nervous, Sol, or my gun"—he tapped the receiver with the barrel—"could go off. Okay. Have a nice day!"

The minute he hung up his smile collapsed. "Tear off the number and put it there," he said to Joe, gesturing to the coffee table. Joe put the slip of paper down and casually went back to the kitchen to put the pad away. He hoped if they behaved well, Dorn would let them start moving around the house by themselves.

When he came back Dorn looked nervous. His eyes were slightly unfocused. "This is what worries me, guys. I've never seen, in a situation like this, on the news or in the movies or anything, where the hostage guy—that's me—didn't get killed. You know, my pal Sol out there is as nice as pie, saying they'll work with me, nobody has to get hurt, but how the hell do I get out of this? The minute I let you guys go, they'll grab me." He paused, like he was hoping for suggestions, but nobody offered any. Joe held back on his idea, which was that Dorn should turn the gun on himself and let them all go free. Joe was amazed that Dorn was discussing things with them, like he thought they were allies and not his victims.

"There's a way to make this work," Dorn said, tapping his gun on the coffee table. "I just have to stall them until I think of what it is. Meanwhile"—he stood up very suddenly—"I guess I have a little score to settle with you, don't I, Chip-boy?" He stood over Nathan. The gun was down at his side, but that didn't stop Joe's heart rate, which had just about slowed down to normal, from cranking up again.

"Look at me when I talk to you!" Dorn roared. "What's your name?"

Nathan slowly tipped his head back to look up the sheer cliff that was Dorn's body. "Nathan Jericho," he said quietly.

"Jericho! You Jewish? Did you think that was real clever, Jericho? Hiding the phone so you could call the cops the minute I was gone? I'll bet you wish I'd gotten away now, don't you?"

Nathan cleared his throat.

"Are you making fun of me, Jericho? Do you think you're smarter than me?"

"I'm not making fun of you. . . ." Nathan said uncertainly. Dorn squatted down, which put him in Nathan's face. He aimed the gun barrel straight into Nathan's crotch. "You follow the news, Jericho? You know what I did to get in this freaking mess?"

"Yeah." Nathan's voice was all breath. "You shot a professor at FAU."

"That's right, Jericho. You know his name?"

They all knew it. It had been in the news for days. "I think it was Rosen." Nathan's voice trembled now.

"That's right, big man. Do you get my point? I'm not all that thrilled with your people right now, you know?"

Nathan gave no response.

"He thought he was better than me." Dorn stood up and paced. Nathan's rigid body slumped and he closed his eyes briefly.

"Do you know what he said to me?" Dorn asked the whole group. "I asked him how I could bring my grade up. I was trying to graduate from college, for God's sake, so I could have a life!" The gun took a wild swing as Dorn gestured. The kids pulled their heads in, like baby chicks when a hawk flies over. "This guy hated everything I wrote. Gave me an F when there was nothing wrong with my spelling or my punctuation or anything *real*. He just didn't like me. He'd write all this crap in the margins like, 'You have failed to support your thesis,' or 'Doubtful conclusions.' Mean things like that. I had to get, like, a C on my final essay or I wouldn't graduate." Dorn was sweating. He wiped his face with his free hand. "I went to him, just like you're supposed to, and I begged him. I said, 'What can I do to be a better writer?' You know what he told me? He said,

'There's nothing you can do, Mr. Dorn. You would have to have a completely different mind to be able to write an acceptable essay.' Did you ever hear anything like that? Is that what a teacher is supposed to say? You're crap and you'll always be crap?"

Joe forced himself to speak. "That was wrong!" he said. At least now Dorn was distracted from being mad at Nathan.

"You're damn right it was wrong!" Dorn paced around a little. "But even after he made that stupid comment, I still thought I could win him over. I worked day and night on that paper. I didn't cheat, I didn't copy an essay from a book, like anybody else would. I went over all my notes from him, trying to figure out what he wanted from me. He said I never exposed my inner self. That I was cold and detached. So I wrote this essay about my father beating the crap out of me when I was ten. I spilled my guts to that man. I must have spent, like, sixty hours writing and rewriting that thing. He hands it back to me with the same old F, but you know what he wrote on it?" Dorn had been pacing in circles but now he came to a dead halt in front of the kids. "His one and only comment? 'Not believable.'" Dorn pounded his chest with his free hand. "It happened to me!" His voice broke a little and Joe thought for a minute Dorn might actually cry.

Dorn walked in circles again, more slowly this time, as if soothing himself. "I knew I wasn't going to graduate, and I didn't have enough money for another semester, and even if I did, there'd be Rosen or some other Rosen standing in my way. I saw my whole life—working at a car wash or something, living in my same crummy apartment with rented furniture. And I realized Rosen had destroyed me." He faced them again. This time his eyes were vulnerable, like a little kid or a very old man. "He robbed me."

He turned away, went to the couch, and sat down. He gestured limply with the gun. "So I bought this."

"It wasn't right, what he did," Joe repeated nervously.

Ramon joined in. "He had it in for you. We've all been there."

Suddenly Tony Ong lifted his head. "I did the same thing," he said to Dorn.

Everybody, including Dorn, jumped, as if a table had spoken. Dorn frowned at him. "You shot one of your teachers?"

Tony shook his head. His eyes were clear and peaceful. "I jumped on him and tried to choke him. He was ten times bigger than me. He was trying to destroy me, too."

Great, Joe thought. Crazy in stereo. Still, the all-important gun hand was completely relaxed now. "What's your name?" Dorn asked.

"Tony. Tony Ong."

Dorn sat back. "So, how'd you beat the rap, Tony? Your parents buy your ass out of it? Or are juveniles allowed to attack people and get away with it?"

"They put me on a psych ward," Tony said.

"Sweet," said Dorn. "Maybe I should start acting crazy. That could be the loophole I've been looking for."

Start acting crazy? Joe thought.

Tony shook his head solemnly. "What they did to me was worse than jail. Way, way worse."

Joe shivered as various possibilities flashed in his mind. He knew Tony wasn't going to tell any details. In fact, this seemed like the most he'd ever opened up. Obviously it took a fellow psycho to draw him out.

"Do you wish you had killed your guy?" Dorn asked.

Tony shook his head. "No."

Dorn sighed. "I wish I hadn't killed Rosen. He deserved it, but I wish I'd never done it. Look at me now." He got up and went over to the pizza pack on the floor, opened it and slid one of the boxes out. "At this point," he continued, "the car wash looks real good." He popped open a box. "You guys hungry? I'm starving."

✗ ✗ ✗

While he ate Dorn turned the TV back on. He liked to watch the coverage of his escape. "I'm a national celebrity," he said. Then they switched to a story on the presidential campaign. "Idiots," he said, hitting the mute button. He took a big bite of his pepperoni slice—from Joe's pizza. "Joe, go get me a beer. And don't mess around too long or I'll shoot your sister." He laughed. Joe didn't.

"We don't have any." Joe sidled up to the box. He'd be damned if he got stuck with that garden special the girls ordered, just because the gunman was eating his pizza.

Dorn obligingly shoved the box over. "You what?"

"We don't have beer. My mom doesn't drink." Joe took a slice and scooted back to the others to eat it. He didn't want to feel like he was turning into Dorn's partner.

"Wine?" Dorn asked. "Like, she must have a bottle of wine she cooks with? Or, you know, an old bottle of rum in the back of the closet somewhere? You must have something. I haven't had a drink for days!"

"Where have you been?" Nathan asked. "Like, were you hiding out somewhere?"

Dorn smiled. He liked to be asked about himself. "In the public library downtown. It's a great place to hide because you can sit in a computer cubicle or put your face in a book. . . . There are always lunch bags around. . . . There's a million places to hide from security. . . ."

"No one saw you?" Francesca said. "With all the publicity, no one recognized your face?"

He laughed. "No. Not one person. A couple of times yesterday, I went up to the information desk and asked a question, just to see what would happen. Maybe if you read too many books you don't watch TV."

"So what made you leave today?" Nathan asked.

"Are you writing a book?" Dorn snapped. His moods

changed so fast. "I was hoping the attention would die down if I waited a few days, but it's just gotten worse. So I figured today I'd get a car and get out of the area."

Elizabeth spoke up. "How'd you get to Coral Springs?"

"I got a ride with this old lady. I was going to shoot her for her car—it was a Z. Don't ask me what she was doing with it, but then . . ." His eyes drifted out to the middle distance. "I couldn't shoot an old lady. She kept talking about stuff and she had one of those key chains with all her grandchildren's names in beads. You know? Hanging out of her ignition. Michael, Amanda, Suzanne, Cassie. I kept looking at that and I thought, I can't drive all the way to the state line looking at their names. . . ." His mind seemed to wander.

Joe was surprised. He had always thought you were either a good person or a bad person. With Dorn it seemed more like a line he could cross and then step back over. He also realized Dorn had told them an important weakness. One that Joe knew all about.

"Boy," he said. "I'm really sorry we don't have anything for you to drink. After all you've been through, that must be rough."

Dorn talked with his mouth full. "What's the matter with your mother? She some kind of religious fanatic?"

"Our father is an alcoholic," Elizabeth said in a voice just this side of snotty. "None of us can stand the sight of alcohol."

Joe cringed. He wasn't sure it was good for her to pour

the salt directly into the wound. But that was her style, what could you do?

"You better get ready to close your eyes then," Dorn told her. "Come on, work with me, Joe. You got Nyquil? Vanilla extract? Rubbing alcohol?"

Diagnosis confirmed. Joe shook his head. He wished they did have something, though. He knew his own father got very temperamental when he couldn't drink. All they needed was a jumpy hallucinating guy with a gun.

Dorn looked flabbergasted. He put his pizza slice down. "Well . . . I guess it's time to find out how room service works." He looked at the slip of paper with the phone number and dialed. "Hey, Sol! My man! Let's see how responsive the special response team really is. I need a six-pack. It's not for me, of course, but the kids would like a drink." He guffawed.

"Mr. Dorn?" Steve said.

"Hold up, Sol." Dorn covered the mouthpiece. "What?"

"Do you want just a six-pack? You don't know how long you'll want to be here."

Joe reached behind Steve and gave him a pat. "Yeah," he said. "Right now, they'll probably give you whatever you want."

Dorn laughed. "You guys are right." He spoke into the receiver again. "Sol? My agent, here, says I should demand a suitcase from you. Make it Coors Light. I don't like to get filled up. And throw in a bottle of Jack Daniels." He listened for a minute. "Okay, but be quick about it. My pizza's getting cold." He hung up and addressed the kids. "He'll call back when they have it. I think I'll pick one of you to go out there in the sniper nest and get it off the porch. Probably you, darling." He waved the gun at Elizabeth. "Not just because you annoy me, but because I know I can trust you not to bolt. If you do, I'll drop Joe here and throw him out after you, even if he is my friend."

"I'll do whatever you tell me to," Elizabeth said through her teeth.

"Good," he said and suddenly glanced up at the TV, grabbed the remote, and turned up the volume. A female reporter was talking over what looked like a prom picture of Dorn. He was wearing a tuxedo and holding an orchid box. ". . . killing spree that began with the brutal shooting of David Rosen, professor of English at Florida Atlantic University. Dorn, the so-called 'Preppy Terrorist,' . . ."

"You guys made up that name!" Dorn argued with the TV. "Look at my bank book and tell me if I'm a preppie!"

". . . Dorn's other victim is forty-two-year-old Phil Hughes of Deerfield Beach, whom Dorn shot while hijacking his car. For unknown reasons, Dorn abandoned the car, a late model Toyota, just a few streets away, making the killing of Hughes especially senseless."

"Like if I kept the car, it would be okay to shoot him!" Dorn responded. He had his feet up on the coffee table. Making himself right at home.

"Why did you ditch the car?" Steve asked.

Dorn grinned, almost sheepishly. "It was a stick. I only know how to drive an automatic."

They all actually laughed at that, including Dorn.

Joe noticed the whole group was getting more relaxed with Dorn now. They were sprawling on the floor, eating pizza, no longer huddled together. People were talking who had been afraid to speak before. He wondered if that was a good thing. Maybe they were getting too comfortable, losing their edge of alertness. If you didn't keep reminding yourself, you could think you were sitting around with a regular guy.

"Look at this piece of crap!" Dorn pointed to the screen. They had cut to a taped interview of Dorn's roommate, Peter Borden. "I can't stand this guy!" Dorn told them.

"Quiet . . ." Bordon was saying, ". . . but always a bit unstable. The type of man who always put one on edge. It was an undefinable . . ."

"Why is he talking like Sigmund Freud?" Dorn complained. "What a show-off. He leaves toenail clippings all over the bathroom floor—" He stopped and looked up. "What was that?"

"What?" Joe's whole body tensed for the thousandth time that night. He had started worrying that the

FBI was going to get fed up and decide to just come in with the guns blasting.

"I heard . . ." Dorn hit the mute button.

"That's a helicopter," Francesca said.

"Maybe they flew your beer in from the Rockies," Steve said, grinning.

"Shhh," Dorn said. "That's scary. It sounds like two helicopters. What are they doing out there?"

Joe tried to picture commandos dropping on the roof and rapelling down the side of the one-story house, but it made no sense.

"I know what it is." Francesca smiled. "Doesn't anybody know? It's right on time."

"What?" Dorn said. "Don't mess around with me!"

"Hit one of the local channels," she said. "Doesn't matter which one. Ten, seven, four, six."

He brought them up in succession. Each one had the same picture: Joe's house in a crisscross network of light beams; barricades at both ends of the street with people standing behind them; police and other cars parked all around; ambulances; every once in a while guys in black running somewhere, some with rifles, some with those see-through shields.

A shiver ran from Joe's feet all the way to the top of his head. "This is weird."

Francesca's father was a local news producer. "Go to CNN," she said confidently. "They'll have this feed by now."

Dorn flipped the channel. There was the same eerie picture of Joe's house.

"We're like, national celebrities," Nathan observed.

Dorn was staring at the screen. "All this," he whispered, "just for me."

For the first time in the forty-five minutes since
Dorn had been holding them hostage, he put the gun
down. Joe knew it was forty-five minutes because he had
been compulsively checking the VCR clock. Some weird
part of him wanted to keep track of how much of the
wrestling show they were missing, as if that mattered now.
Fusion was very predictable, and Joe knew that now, just
before nine o'clock, something big would happen, because
a competing show came on another network at nine.
Maybe Jack Shine would announce he was quitting the
business. He did that quite often. Maybe he would issue a
challenge to The Siberian Savage or El Tigre.

Joe had read a book in school about POWs in Vietnam.
One guy said he kept his sanity by pretending he had
bought a mansion in England. He imagined the floor plans,
bought furniture, designed formal gardens—all in his
mind. Joe had a feeling his interest in wrestling was like
that. Maybe everybody needed at least one unreal world
where they could escape when things got bad.

The gun made a clink on the glass table. Joe immediately glanced at the other kids and saw that little looks were shooting all around. Then Nathan made a quick chopping motion with his hand, which Joe took to mean, "Stop making eye contact. Don't let him realize we've noticed what he did."

"We've learned there could be as many as ten children inside the house," a reporter was saying. Then there was some speculation as to why Dorn had picked this particular house. That was something Joe would like to have known. He felt like maybe God was pissed off at him about something, or He wouldn't have let this happen.

"I wonder how they got the pizza guy out in such a hurry," Dorn was saying, as he scanned the TV view of the driveway and the street.

Joe wondered the same thing. Where was the ambulance? Why wasn't the pizza truck somewhere on the scene? Joe couldn't believe the FBI guys throwing up a perimeter would care about moving a stray vehicle.

"Are you sure you killed him?" Steve asked.

Dorn stared at him. "Pretty sure . . ." he said. "I shot him in the chest from, like, two feet away! I mean, I didn't wait around to—"

"When did you take his clothes off him?" Steve seemed to be getting into it, like he was at a murder mystery party.

"Before I shot him, obviously!" Dorn said. "I wouldn't come up to your door with a big, bloody hole in my shirt." His eyes unfocused again. "What happened was, I was walking in your neighborhood, looking for a car to hijack, and I saw the pizza truck pull in here and I realized it would be a great way to get into a house. So I just jumped aboard and he started panicking and offering me his crappy little pencil case full of money. . . ."

OUR DRIVERS ALWAYS CARRY LESS THAN $50, Joe remembered from the coupons.

"And I told him to strip." Dorn chuckled. "That was pretty funny, actually. 'Cause he was just a kid. He didn't look much older than you guys. I'm sure he thought I was going to do something perverted to him." Dorn was really tickled by the thought. He laughed, even though no one else was joining in. "So anyway, I put on the uniform, shot him, reached behind him to get the pizzas, and came to your door."

"He could have survived," Steve said. "He could have maybe driven out of the neighborhood and called 911."

"Maybe he recognized you," Francesca said. "That would explain why the Special Response Team got here so fast."

"Yeah . . ." Dorn was talking to himself now. "Maybe I should have shot him in the head. . . ."

Joe's brain just had time to register, with a lurch of dread, that Ramon had made a movement in his peripheral vision, a glide, a kind of forward shift, like a cat getting ready to pounce. Joe's stomach twisted and his mind said, Oh, no! and there was the image of Ramon's runner's body, sprinting to the coffee table in three loping bounds. His long black hair swirled behind him like a flag. There were Nathan and Steve, both reaching out their hands into empty space as if to grab him back. There was Dorn, looking hurt and betrayed, tackling the gun just seconds before Ramon got there. Ramon's dive, like a runner trying to steal second, ended up a bumpy crash landing that bounced him off the table and onto the floor where the gun barrel came to meet him. Then Joe's mind jammed into a prayer, *Don't let him shoot, don't let him shoot.*

After that, there was just the flash of searchlights and the roar of the helicopters and the drone of CNN, as Dorn, trembling and furious, held the shaky gun to Ramon's head. One of Ramon's hands fluttered up toward his face, as if to make a shield. His voice was a thin wail, with a Spanish accent Joe had never heard before. "Oh, please!"

Joe had the horrible wish that if Dorn was going to shoot him, he'd hurry up and do it, because the suspense was doing something awful to Joe's insides, stretching them like a rubber band.

Oblivious to the situation, CNN babbled on. "The owner of the home has been identified as Kathy Anderson, a school psychologist, whose son and daughter were hosting a party for their friends when this nightmare began."

Some party, Joe thought.

"Get up," Dorn growled at Ramon.

Shaking like a stop sign in a hurricane, Ramon first let himself fall on his rear end, then got on all fours, then stood. His hair fell forward, obscuring his face from Joe's view.

Dorn's eyes were cold and predatory. He picked up the remote and hit the mute button. Now there was nothing but the chug of the helicopters.

"What's your name?" Dorn asked.

Ramon's voice was like wind in dry branches. "Ramon Guerrero."

✗ ✗ ✗

Joe remembered the first time he met Ramon. There had been a crowd gathering in a remote corner of the school yard, and Nathan and Joe had followed the flow to see the new kid, Ramon Guerrero. Majestic in a black T-shirt and jeans, wearing a rainbow-colored headband, he crouched in the dust, lighting a stub of a candle, sheltering the flame with his long, slender fingers. The focused, intense look in Ramon's eyes suggested he was going to perform a religious ritual, but then he glanced at the crowd, grinned, and began to pass his hand slowly back and forth through the flame.

There were some mild gasps of wonder, but then Steve spoke up. "It's just because he keeps his hand moving. You can't feel anything that way."

Ramon fixed his dark eyes on Steve, then he looked down, almost lovingly, at the fire and brought his hand to a complete stop over the flame. Seconds passed. Smoke furled around Ramon's hand. Several kids, including Tony Ong, walked away, holding their stomachs or making gagging sounds. Joe thought he could smell something like bacon cooking. But Steve, Joe, and Nathan all moved in closer.

Finally Ramon pulled his hand away and displayed a

red, scorched palm as he calmly blew out the candle.

"How did you do that?" Steve asked.

Ramon blew on his hand several times. It looked like it was swelling. "You challenged me. I had no choice."

Nathan's eyebrows shot up. "So if I told you you couldn't survive jumping out of a sixth-story window, what would you do then?"

Ramon made his face mock-serious. "Please don't tell me that," he said.

✗ ✗ ✗

"Cuban?" Dorn demanded, as if this would add to Ramon's crimes.

Ramon reached up slowly and gathered his hair back from his face. "I was born here. My family is from Colombia."

"Colombia!" Dorn said. "What, are they a bunch of drug lords?"

"Sir?"

Dorn enunciated carefully. "What does your father do?"

"He's an EMT?" Ramon said as if guessing.

Dorn barked a laugh. "That could come in handy for you, Ramon. Are you his only son?"

Ramon was getting pale. Apparently he, like Joe, thought that question was to decide if Ramon was expendable.

"Yes, sir, I am," he said, lying. He had three brothers.

"Hmm," Dorn said. He pretended to think, scratching his chin with the barrel of the gun. "Well, Ramon, I think you watch too many Chuck Norris movies."

"Sir?"

"Thinking you can be a hero and grab the gun? If I was the only son of a proud immigrant, I'd take better care of my life than that."

Joe's stomach was churning. He wished he hadn't eaten so much pizza.

Ramon closed his eyes briefly. "Please, Mr. Dorn. I'm sorry. That was stupid."

Dorn smiled. "Are you really sorry, Ramon? Really, really sorry?"

Ramon's voice rose to a wail. "Yes! Yes!"

Dorn made little circles in the air with the gun barrel. "I think you're just saying you're sorry because you don't want me to shoot you. I don't really feel your sincerity."

"Please, Mr. Dorn. Please."

Dorn's face was flushed, almost like this was getting him excited. Joe had to close his eyes for a second. He hated Dorn so much, it was like an unbearable pounding in his head. He didn't want that to show on his face.

"Stand on one foot," Dorn said.

"Sir?"

The gun jabbed the air. "Stand on one foot, Ramon. I'm the boss, *comprende*? Don't ask questions."

Ramon's whole body trembled. Awkwardly, he bent his left knee and lifted the foot off the ground. He wobbled, trying to keep his balance.

"Okay, now put your arms out to your sides." Dorn grinned.

Ramon closed his eyes again. He took a deep breath. He raised both arms, holding them out like a scarecrow. The wobble in his balance improved slightly. Joe was glad it wasn't Tony Ong being asked to do this.

"Now, Ramon, the reason you're doing this is because I have the gun, *comprende?*"

Ramon nodded.

"Answer me out loud."

"Yes, sir."

"Repeat after me. 'The guy with the gun gives all the orders.'"

"The guy with the gun gives all the orders." Ramon tilted, but managed to correct himself.

"If he says, 'Strip naked and stand on your head,' I will strip naked and stand on my head."

Joe heard a funny gulping sound next to him. He looked at Tony and he was weeping.

"If he says, 'Strip naked and stand on your head,' I will strip naked and stand on my head," Ramon said.

"I am afraid of him!"

Ramon's face flushed with anger. "I am afraid of him."

"I will not pull crazy stunts that could get me and my friends killed."

"I will not pull crazy stunts that could get me and my friends killed."

"My father is a stupid wetback."

"My father . . ." Another deep breath. He shook his head no.

Dorn and his gun lunged forward a few inches. "Say it!"

A tear ran down Ramon's face. He whispered, ". . . is a stupid . . . wetback."

Dorn chuckled. "Okay, Ramon, that was pretty good. You can sit down now."

Joe looked away while Ramon walked toward him and sat down.

Dorn got up slowly and circled the room, speaking to each kid in turn. "We don't want any more of that kind of thing, do we, kids?" He pressed the gun, briefly, to the side of Ramon's head. "Because this isn't a Chuck Norris movie, and none of you little lamebrains are heroes." He took a step and shoved the gun at Steve's head. Then he stepped again and did it to Tony, whose soft wailing rose a little, then fell. It was like a sick game of Duck, Duck, Goose. "You guys have to remember . . ." The first inch of the barrel disappeared into Francesca's hair. "I've already killed two or three people." Nathan. "I don't care about any of you. I don't have anything to lose." Elizabeth. "If any of you pulls something again, I'm just going to empty this gun into all of you and wait for the boys in black to come in and finish me off." Joe. The same as before, only now the barrel wasn't warm. It just felt heavy and big and explosive. "So . . ."

The phone jangled. Dorn was startled and the gun barrel scraped Joe's scalp. *Hail Mary* . . . But the gun didn't go off. Dorn went to the phone. "Remember what I said," he warned as he picked up the handset. "Hello? . . . What are you talking about? . . . You're crazy! I'm not flustered. You sound flustered, Sol. The kids and I were just playing Simon Says. It's like a big slumber party in here." He laughed at something the FBI agent said. "Well, that's good news. Tell your sharpshooters I'm sending a kid out for it, so they should hold their fire. Put it on the welcome mat, right by the front door, ring the bell, and move back. I can see you guys on CNN, so don't do anything cute. Hey! How come they don't ask you for an interview, Sol? Aren't you high enough up in the company?" Dorn laughed at something that was said. "Okay. Now remember, I've got a gun on this kid, so don't try to grab him. Oh, sure, I trust you just like you trust me." He laughed and hung up. "I wonder how many classes those guys have to take to be so charming to a guy they want to kill?" he said. "Good news, kids! The liquor is here. Let's see, which one of you wants to go out and be cannon fodder? Joe? I know I can trust you. . . ." Joe felt a twinge of something like guilt. "But I think you deserve a rest. Maybe your sister. Or Mr. Jericho over there. Both of them really annoy me. That way, if there's an accident . . ."

The doorbell rang. Someone brushed their body against the front door. Everyone looked at the live feed from CNN. Two figures in black were rapidly backing up from the door. The announcer tried to analyze. "They've put some kind of package on the porch. It could be tear gas or . . ."

"Better not be," Dorn said. "I can't believe how little these media guys know! Okay, I've made my decision. Ramon, you want to be a hero. You go out there. You've got nice, quick reflexes, and you know that if you screw up, I'll waste you. Get up."

Ramon, who had probably never stopped shaking from the last incident, hauled himself to his feet, swaying slightly. He had what wrestlers call spaghetti legs.

"Come on, don't horse around. Go to the door, pronto! You other guys, move away from the TV. Come back this way a little. Don't want you in the crossfire." Dorn shepherded them all back toward the center of the room, then urged Ramon toward the door. "Okay, light-foot. You just dash out there, get my beer, and come right back in. I see one false move and I'll sacrifice a hostage. Okay?"

"Okay."

"Okay," Dorn said. "Go!"

Ramon opened the door. The helicopter clatter intensified and a cool breeze passed over Joe's face. Freedom air. Joe looked at the TV screen to see the outside view.

"Apparently one of the children is coming out," CNN said. "We don't really know why. It must be connected to the package on the porch. Now—oh, my God!"

Joe couldn't believe what he was seeing either. Ramon had meekly bent to pick up the case, and then sabot-kicked the door shut with his foot and took off running full speed. He only got about six feet from the door when a man in black dove from the bushes, tackled him, and dragged him to cover.

Ramon was free.

Ramon was safe.

Right after the door slam, Dorn had started yelling, "No! No! No!" He pounded his gun against the floor in frustration.

Elizabeth hissed. "Good!"

Dorn aimed at her. "You shut up!" His words were slurred with rage.

He got up and walked around the carpet, swearing and swearing. Talking about Ramon and his family, Latino people in general, Judas, God, and the Devil.

Calm down, please, Joe thought. He was angry with Ramon, too. It was like he'd abandoned them. Or, no, it was that this wasn't fair. Ramon had done two stupid reckless things. The *wrong* things. And he'd been rewarded! He should be dead. Joe felt terrible for having such a feeling, but . . . what if they were all doing the wrong thing by cooperating and waiting? What if they were all going to be slaughtered and only Ramon, who knew how to take risks, was going to live?

". . . amazing rescue of one of the children," said CNN. "We know now there are six left in the house. . . ."

The telephone rang.

Dorn's eyes narrowed. "Oh, you dirty . . ." He picked up the handset. "I didn't like that, Sol! I didn't like that at all! I've got a real strong urge to shoot one of my hostages just to show you guys how angry I am! I'm tired of everyone treating me like a clown!" He listened for a minute. "No, no, I know he did it. No, I know that. It's just that I think you're laughing at me. I think you put that stuff on the porch because you knew I'd send a kid out. Well, at least I learn from my mistakes. Hold on and watch. . . ." He put the handset down and headed straight for Joe.

Since the last thing he'd said was about wasting a kid for the heck of it, Joe had a ferocious struggle with his bladder, which he barely managed to win. Dorn hauled him up by his collar and dragged him toward the door. "Hey!" Joe said, his voice sounding about six years old.

"Don't you hurt my brother!" Elizabeth shouted.

The gun swung like a boom toward her. "I told you to shut up and I mean it! This is your last warning. Come on!" he said to Joe, dragging him to the front door. He pushed it open and went out, shoving Joe ahead of him. The phrase "human shield" popped into Joe's mind.

They were on the porch. Joe was breathing the dark, cool, freedom air. Searchlights blinded him and the helicopter noises were frightening. Wind from the propellers burned his eyes. Joe thought he heard a click that could have been a rifle. Joe felt a strange rush of awe. *I have a pistol to my head and rifles aimed at me*, he thought. *And an hour ago I was worried about whether I had the right kind of sodas for my party.*

Dorn held Joe's collar in one fist and kept the gun at the back of his head with the other. "Pick up the stuff. Fast!"

There was a case of beer and a bottle of Jack Daniels. Joe bent awkwardly, choking a little, and struggled to pick it all up without dropping anything.

"See, Sol?" Dorn shouted into the darkness. "I learn from my mistakes. This is the right way to do it, isn't it?"

There was no answer. "Come on," he growled, dragging Joe backward over the threshold, back out of the freedom air, into the jail. Joe felt tears streaming down his own face, even though he hadn't known he was crying.

Dorn pulled the door shut and exhaled. "Good, Joe! You're the only one I can count on!"

Joe set the liquor on the hall rug, sat down on the floor, and gave in to some baby-style, all-out bawling. He didn't care anymore.

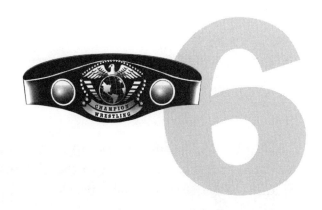

Joe knew the precise moment when his feelings for Francesca had changed. It happened a month ago when Elizabeth got her telescope.

Francesca and Elizabeth became best friends last year, so Francesca had been around the house a lot. Joe's earliest feelings for her had been a kind of abstract admiration. She was so graceful, so precise. It seemed to Joe that she came from a cleaner, better world than the one he lived in, where his mother rooted through the clothes hamper on Monday morning, looking for a blouse to wear to work that wasn't too dirty.

Francesca could eat a whole ice-cream bar without rushing or dripping. She had a straight-A average, even in the classes she claimed to hate. She was a gymnast, the favorite sport of perfectionists, and she played first clarinet in the orchestra. She never lost her temper or said a bad word. She said, "No, thank you," if candy was passed around. You could just look at Francesca and know that even though both her parents worked, somehow her house was spotless, nutritious meals hit the table every night at six, and the whole family probably watched public TV all evening long. You knew that ants had never swarmed into their kitchen because somebody let a banana get too ripe on the windowsill.

All of this fascinated Joe in the same way math fascinated him. He was drawn to the idea that there were paradises of perfection in the universe—places where order and simplicity ruled.

At the same time, Joe couldn't help noticing that his sister's friend was very pretty. And if a very pretty girl is walking around a guy's house on a regular basis, he's going to notice. Francesca had some kind of floral cologne that would waft into Joe's room when she walked down the hall. Her voice was as low and melodious as the clarinet she played. He remembered when she and Elizabeth had been practicing *Peter and the Wolf* in Elizabeth's room. He listened through the wall—Francesca playing her little cat theme over and over somehow summed up everything she was: sleek, deft, and coy.

But even all of this didn't prompt him to have a crush on her. It was a kind of impersonal worship he felt for her. She was from another world, not because of her culture, but because she was so perfect, and Joe felt so flawed. He had nothing to say to her.

Then Elizabeth got the telescope. It was thanks to Joe that she got it. The orchestra was selling chocolate bars so they could go to summer music camp. And Elizabeth's sales technique was awful. She presented the customers with negatives up front: "It has to be cash, I can't take a check," or "You just want one bar? Most people buy at least two." What she lacked in sales savvy, though, she made up for in delegating ability. After one day of getting doors slammed in her face, she came straight to Joe and said, "Look, I need to cash in on your insincere charm. If you sell my candy bars for me and I win a prize, we can pick out something together from the catalog and share it."

Joe saw it as win-win. The incentive prize catalog had some awesome stuff, he actually liked to go door-to-door and talk to people, and the thought of having Elizabeth out of his hair for four weeks while she went to band camp was a bonus.

So Joe went door to door. Big-time. He played a variety of angles: Charm—"You can't be old enough to be her mother. . . ."; Temptation—"I've tasted them. It's like dark, Belgian chocolate. . . ."; Pity— "Since our father left, music is the only thing that makes my sister happy." In four weeks, Elizabeth set a school record for chocolate sales, and Elizabeth and Joe happily perused the first-prize section of the incentive catalog. With a surprisingly minimal amount of debate they agreed on the Questar 250, a low-power tele-scope by Kitt Peak standards, but way better than binoculars.

It came by UPS a month ago. It drove them crazy all afternoon because there was nothing to do but set it up and wait for it to get dark. While they were waiting, they agreed to invite Nathan and Francesca over that night to look at the half-moon. Nathan had plans, but Francesca accepted.

Joe saw how she looked in white shorts and a matching top that glowed in the moonlight. They set the telescope up in the driveway. Joe realized Francesca's cologne was the same as the night-blooming flowers by the front door. White jasmine.

"Okay," he said, feeling lightheaded and silly. "Which neighbor's house should we point it at first?"

Elizabeth checked and rechecked the legs of the tripod, making sure everything was stable. "I'm gonna tell Mom you said that."

Joe opened his mouth to fire something back. Then he glanced at Francesca, who was smiling at him, and he lost his train of thought. "Let Francesca look first," he said. "She's our guest."

Elizabeth gave him a strange look and Francesca took a step back. "No, no. It belongs to you guys."

Joe gently pulled Elizabeth away. "I insist," he said. Elizabeth stepped on his foot. He couldn't tell if it was an accident.

Francesca tilted the telescope toward the moon and looked in the viewer. She fiddled with the focus. "I don't see anything," she said. "Am I doing it right?"

Joe stepped up into her jasmine aura and repositioned the scope. "Now?"

"I . . . oh!" Francesca jumped back as one leg of the tripod collapsed and the telescope crashed on the blacktop.

The mirrors, Joe thought. *It's a goner.*

"Oh!" Francesca's hands covered the lower part of her face as she stared at the fallen instrument. "Oh, no, oh, no, oh, no!" Her wails echoed inside her hands.

Joe felt a little scared of her as he rushed to make it right. He pulled the telescope up and reset the legs. Maybe if it still worked she would calm down.

Francesca backed up as if the telescope was hitting her with powerful rays. "Oh, how could I be so clumsy! Oh, God!"

"Francesca, it's okay," Elizabeth was saying as Joe frantically tried to see through the telescope. "It was an accident."

The moon appeared in the lens in all its ripe, fuzzy glory.

"It's okay!" Joe called. "It still works. No harm done." He looked up.

Francesca sat on the blacktop, rocking back and forth, still moaning. In the moonlight he saw the sparkle of tears on her face. "How could that have happened?" she said, sobbing, as Elizabeth crouched down beside her. "How could I have done that?"

"It's okay," Elizabeth said. "Didn't you hear him? It's not broken. It's okay."

Francesca crumpled forward. "I'm so clumsy! I'm so stupid!"

Joe's mind raced to understand what was going on. The crisis was over; what was wrong with her? Was she just one of those people who, once they lost it, took a long time to recover? He kneeled on the other side of her. "It doesn't matter," he said, putting his hand on her heaving shoulder.

"But I was trying to be careful." She looked at Joe with pleading eyes. "I was trying so hard."

Suddenly Joe understood the blessing of a mother who didn't do the wash on time and left bananas on the windowsill. "You try too hard," he told her.

She buried her face in his shoulder. "I know," she said, and that was the minute Joe fell in love. Because now he knew he had something to offer her.

X X X

Joe looked at her now, sitting on the floor with her back straight, her eyes tranquil, her hands folded neatly. He realized she'd had nothing to eat but a few sips of cranberry juice. He wondered if this situation was worse for a person like her, who kept so much of her life in control. "Eat something, Francesca," he said softly, ignoring the fact that everyone swung their heads to look at him.

"Yeah." She ducked her head. Slowly she drew one of the pizza boxes toward her and picked off a sliver of green pepper.

"That's not eating," Joe said. "Have some pepperoni." He shoved his box toward her. "It's great. It's made from hundreds of discarded animal parts."

She giggled. "My mother would have a fit if I ate one of those things." Her mother was a dietician.

"Francesca," Joe said, glancing at Dorn. "It doesn't matter."

She looked up at him, taking in the full impact of what he said. Then she smiled, as if she realized Joe was trying to take care of her. "It doesn't matter, does it?" she said.

He shook his head no. She took a huge bite and even let the sauce run down her chin for a quarter of a second before reaching for a napkin. "That's the best thing I've ever tasted," she said.

Nathan opened his mouth to say something and Joe was sure he was now busted. But whatever Nathan was going to say, he forgot it as he whirled toward the television screen.

He'd heard his mother's voice.

". . . don't even know what's going on! They came to the door—we just live a few doors down—he was just going to Joe's house to watch TV!"

Joe had never seen Nathan's mother so disheveled. Her hair was sticking out funny on one side and she wore no makeup. She had on a pink nightgown stuffed into a pair of jeans. Nathan's little sisters, Lanie and Rachel, were hanging on to Mrs. Jericho's legs like little marsupials, crying with their mouths wide open.

"Oh, God," Nathan said.

"Who's that?" Dorn put down his beer and reached for the remote. He turned the volume up.

"It's my mother," Nathan said. "Why did she bring the girls over here? They shouldn't be seeing this stuff! There's guys with guns out there!"

"Take it easy," Joe said. "There're probably guys with guns all over the neighborhood. Maybe she thought they'd be more scared if she left them alone at your house."

"Oh, yeah?" Nathan said. "Look at them!"

"This is a good neighborhood!" Mrs. Jericho was wailing. "I don't see how this could have happened here!"

Dorn chuckled. Nathan turned as if to attack, and Joe literally threw his arms around his friend to stop him. Nathan wriggled loose like an angry child, but he stayed put. "Get the cameras off her," he yelled at the screen. "She's raving!"

"Ramon probably gave the names and numbers of who was in here," Francesca said. "So now they're being notified."

"And your mom's the closest so she got here first," Joe said.

"I'll bet they haven't been able to find Mom!" Elizabeth grabbed Joe's arm. "She's on her way home from that workshop. She'll pull up to the house and see this!" She gestured wildly at the TV.

"Yeah." Joe swallowed around the lump in his throat. He didn't want his mother to know. He wished she could stay in that writing class forever and be happy.

"Look at what they're doing to her!" Nathan was picking frantically at his cuticles. "They're blinding her with those lights and sticking those microphones in her face. They're scaring my sisters!" He whirled on Dorn. "How could you do this!"

Dorn immediately pointed the gun at him. "Hey! Hey! Hey! You keep quiet, Jericho, or I'll really give your mother something to cry about!"

"We've got . . . who have we got?" The reporter was pushing Nathan's mother to the side, looking at something off-camera. "Mrs. Anderson? This is the homeowner? Yes! Get her over here!"

"There's Mom!" Elizabeth cried.

A tall African-American man stepped into the camera shot. "Turn that off," he said forcefully. "I need to talk to Mrs. Anderson." It was a beautiful, deep voice that Joe recognized.

"That's Solomon Page!"

Page whisked Joe's mother away. The camera, though, stayed with a long shot of them talking; Joe's mom crying and gesturing toward the house, like she wanted to go in. Page gave her a handkerchief.

"There are truly wrenching moments in a crisis like this," the reporter said in a fake-sad voice. "The parents, reacting to the news, learning their children—innocent children—are being held at gunpoint. . . ."

"Okay, okay, you get your award," Dorn muttered.

Solomon Page looked up at the camera that was tracking him. He made an abrupt gesture to someone off screen.

The next thing Joe heard was a loud buzzing sound. The screen turned to snow.

"Did they cut the cable?" Francesca said.

Joe felt frantic. He couldn't see his mom anymore. He thought of Dorothy looking in the witch's crystal ball, *Auntie Em! Auntie Em!*

Dorn flipped through the local channels trying to get a picture back. "What did they do that for?"

"I think the FBI cut them off," Francesca said. "They probably didn't want you to see . . . you know, where their men are . . . around . . ."

Dorn turned the TV completely off. "Either that or

they're getting ready to do something!" Dorn cried. The whites showed all around his eyes. "I swear if they storm in here, I'll take all of you out before they get me!"

Tony started to cry again.

"They just don't want you to see their positions!" Francesca argued. "That's all."

"You don't know that!" Dorn shouted.

"I do! My father works in television," she yelled back, "I'm surprised they let us watch as long as they did!"

Dorn was panting, staring at the door. "I liked it better when I could see. . . ."

"Me too," Joe said.

For a few seconds they all stared at the hard, opaque door, listening to the sounds of the helicopters slicing back and forth over the roof as searchlights swept into the room like lightsabers.

Joe crawled on his hands and knees over to Tony and put his arms around him.

Dorn popped open a beer, juggling the gun in his palm. He took a sip, then lowered the can. "They wouldn't put something in this, would they?"

Joe didn't like this new mood of Dorn's. All jittery and paranoid. It had started when the TV went off. The lack of background noise made them all too aware of the helicopters cruising over the roof.

"How could they?" Nathan said. "You just opened it. They can't inject something into a metal can."

"Maybe the FBI makes this stuff in a warehouse somewhere." Dorn peered at the can.

Francesca spoke up. "How would they know you were going to ask for beer? They can't manufacture everything every hostage guy is going to want."

"The government has a lot of resources," Dorn argued. "One of you taste it first."

Steve's hand shot out. "Finally. An assignment with my name on it."

Elizabeth turned to him. "Don't drink that, Steve. It isn't good for you."

Steve, who was famous for being good-natured even with three different coaches screaming in his ears, somehow switched his twinkly blue eyes into laser beams, boring into Elizabeth. "Sitting in this room with a gun on me isn't good for me! This may be my last chance to drink beer, since I'm not betting on my graduation party right now!"

Dorn stared at him, like Steve had been rude to point out that he was threatening to kill them. "Here." He nudged the beer almost gently into Steve's outstretched hand.

Joe wondered if Steve had had beer before. It seemed like more than just eager curiosity. He looked like a guy under stress who knew what his drug of choice could do for him. Like an expert, Steven tipped it up and took five big swallows. His Adam's apple pulled like a rake, hurrying the liquid down his throat. Suddenly Joe wondered about Steve's legendary good nature, the high color in his cheeks, his trouble getting to school on time. *Could you be an alcoholic at thirteen?*

✗ ✗ ✗

Joe remembered a phone call he'd gotten from Steve one night.

"Joe? You gotta help me!"

"Who is this?"

"Who is this? This is Steve. Your old best friend buddy Steve. I'm in trouble, Joe, you gotta help me. Can I sleep over at your house?"

It all made sense now: the slurred consonants, the loud roaring tone. At the time, though, all Joe had registered was a vague uneasiness. "Why would you want to do that?"

"I can't go home. I'm . . . sick and my mom will kill me. Joe, please."

"Where's Ramon?" Ramon was Steve's official best friend and Joe knew Steve crashed over there all the time.

"He won't let me. He thinks he'll get in trouble. Joe, I don't want to get anybody in trouble, but I don't know what to do! My mom—"

"Steve, if you're sick, why would she be mad at you? It doesn't make sense. She's probably worried about you. Where are you anyway?"

"Salevin—" Steve broke off and coughed loudly.

"Where?"

"Seven. Aleven. By that street, you know? The one with the tree?"

"Steve, quit goofing around and go home. I've gotta go."

"No! No! No! Don't hang up. That was all my change!"

"Good. Then go home." Joe hung up.

How stupid could a person be? Joe had forgotten that incident the minute it happened. Had told himself Steve was playing around, making a crank call. Joe wondered if he had deliberately ignored the signals he knew so well.

✗ ✗ ✗

"Joey-bear, run down to the corner and get your dad a beer, okay, buddy?"

Joe remembered holding a book up in front of his face. He hated seeing his father sprawled on the couch, pretending to be a sports fan. The Dolphins were playing, but Joe knew his dad had zoned out of the game a quarter ago.

"You have one there you haven't finished," Joe muttered.

His father picked up the bottle and swung it back and forth, like a bell. "But it's almost gone, Joey!" he said theatrically.

Elizabeth walked in then. She descended like a hawk on the empties, gathering them up. "Sit up!" she said. "Mom will be home any minute."

"Don't talk to him like that!" Joe shouted. "He's your father!"

"Yeah!" said Mr. Anderson.

"Look at him!" Elizabeth continued. "He's disgusting!"

Joe jumped up. "You take that back!"

"Kids!" Mr. Anderson put his hands to his temples. "Guys!"

Then the front door opened. Joe's mom walked in, arms full of groceries. Her eyes scanned the room, taking it all in. She never broke stride on her way to the kitchen, just called over her shoulder, "Running out of second chances, Joe."

Joe flinched, as he always did, even though he knew she meant Joe Sr. and not him.

Elizabeth trailed after her, carrying the empties. Joe left the room when his father started to cry.

X X X

Dorn watched Steve for a reaction to FBI poison, then cautiously drank from his own can. His Adam's apple made the same greedy motions. "Oh, that's better," he sighed, closing his eyes. "You guys sure you don't want one? It's really good for your nerves."

Apparently everyone else wanted to leave their nerves the way they were.

"Now, I've got to think," Dorn said. "That little bastard Ramon is out there spilling his guts to the men in black, probably drawing a whole map of the house for them. . . ." His eyes widened. "We have to move. If they know where I am, they can shoot at me. Let's go down the hall to that big bedroom." He gestured with the gun. "Joe, you take the phone. Steve can carry the supplies."

Steve laughed. He had already finished his can of beer. "Do we get a tip?" He hefted the case and the bottle of Jack.

Joe picked up the phone and led the way down the hall to his mother's room. They shuffled behind him like a nervous herd of sheep. He flipped on the lights and turned to find Nathan reaching out to stop him. "You just told them what room we moved to!" Nathan sighed, exasperated.

Dorn swore. "I hate having to think all the time. Joe, go turn on the lights in every room in the house and come right back."

Joe tried not to show his surprise. Dorn was trusting

him to walk around the house alone? Had the beer made him that sloppy or did he just think Joe was too chicken to try to escape? Joe's heart began to hammer in his chest. He went across the hall and flipped on the light in Elizabeth's room. Her mobile of tropical fish nodded in the breeze from the air-conditioning.

Joe walked slowly out of Dorn's line of sight and flipped on the light in his own room. Jack Shine gazed solemnly down from the wall. Joe had always imagined the poster telling him to have courage. He sat in front of it some afternoons, as if it were an icon, especially when he'd had a bad day at school. Jack Shine's expression always seemed to tell Joe, *You're stronger than you think. Just like me.*

Joe began to edge toward the foyer. *I can walk out the door like Ramon and be free. I gained his trust by doing all the right things and this is my reward.* He paused to flick on the light in the second bathroom, the one he and Elizabeth shared. For some reason, an old memory flashed in his mind, of standing on the stepstool when he was six and holding Elizabeth around the waist, so she could fill something with water. What was it? A water pistol? A balloon? *Why am I thinking about that now? It's time to run!*

He crept up on the front door like an animal stalking its prey. His chest was so tight, he thought he was having a heart attack. He stood in front of the door listening to the roar of helicopters outside, where freedom was, but . . .

Your sister is back there with Dorn. Your best friend. Your brand-new girlfriend. Are you going to abandon them?

But in an emergency, didn't you save whoever you could? Ramon had an opportunity and took it. Why shouldn't Joe?

"Hurry up, Joe!" Dorn called.

Joe touched the wood of the door. It was smooth and smelled like furniture polish. He pictured the FBI agents out there, big strong guys who couldn't wait to catch him and pull him to safety. In his mind they all looked like his father.

He would be so angry if you betrayed him. He might kill somebody.

Joe felt an unexpected tear leak out of his right eye and slide down his face. He stepped back from the door. Maybe survival wasn't the first commandment. Maybe there was something else that had to be preserved at all costs. He went to the kitchen and flipped on the lights.

When he appeared in the bedroom doorway, Nathan, Francesca, and Elizabeth all stared at him like he was an idiot. And maybe he was. Steven, tipping up his beer can, was oblivious.

"Good boy, Joe, I can really depend on you," Dorn said.

Joe sat down on the floor under the Norman Bates poster, squinting against the rest of his tears, ignoring his friends' stares, wondering what kind of freak he really was.

The group had already made camp in Mrs. Anderson's bedroom. The drapes were tightly shut and they all sat on the floor, apparently using the bed as a bunker between them and the window. Dorn sat with his back against the door, like a guard. Both he and Steve were on their second beers.

"So what's the deal with you kids?" Dorn asked. "Are you part of some multi-cultural program the school system is forcing down your parents' throats?"

"What the hell do you mean by that?" Francesca blurted out, then covered her mouth with both hands. Elizabeth and Nathan both laughed.

Surprisingly, Dorn laughed, too. The beer was definitely chilling him. "Come on, guys!" He counted on his fingers. "A Hispanic, a Jew, an Asian, a black, Catholic twins and then Steve here representing the WASPs. You want to tell me you're all friends just by accident?"

"How do you know we're Catholic?" Elizabeth demanded. Joe wished she wouldn't use that tone of voice.

"Mommy has a rosary in her worthless jewelry collection." Dorn took a swig and laughed. "Actually all the cheap jewelry was a clue. I bet if we were at Nathan's house, I would have made out like a bandit!"

"Hey!" Francesca said. "We have to put up with you holding a damn gun on us. Do we have to put up with racist remarks, now, too?"

Dorn chuckled. "Wooo! Feisty!" His eyes shone in a way Joe didn't like. "I'm not a racist, honey. Really. Want me to prove it to you?"

"We're all in the same gifted program," Joe said quickly. "That's how we got to be friends. It is just an accident that we're . . . diverse."

"Yeah, right," Dorn tossed his empty at the wicker wastebasket, missed it by a mile, and started beer number three. "You guys don't know it but your school probably got a grant to make sure their gifted program was . . . diverse." He smirked.

Obviously Dorn had pushed Francesca too far. "Listen, you! You wanna know what my IQ is? You want to play a game of chess with me?"

Dorn leered at her. "I'll tell you what I'd like to—"

"The real thing that makes us friends," Joe said frantically, "is that we're all fans of Pro-Wrestling!"

"Speak for yourself!" said Elizabeth.

Joe was sweating. "We all watch this show every Friday night. Friday Night Fusion."

"Yeah, yeah. I remember the fag poster in your room. Don't you guys know it's all fake? How can you be smart kids and get taken in by that crap? Those guys are just actors."

"We know that." Joe was actually panting in his efforts to drag the conversation away from explosive areas. *This is why I had to stay.* "But it's like a comic book. You know? Even when it's silly, you get caught up in the feelings. There's always some little guy, going against the odds. . . ."

Steve pitched his beer can in a perfect arc into the wastebasket, then cautiously reached and took his third beer, shooting nervous glances at Dorn as if he thought he might bite. "Wait a minute, Joe," Steve said. "That's the story line you like because your hero is that washed-up dork who should have retired ten years ago. But there're new guys in the sport who are really big and buff. . . ."

"They abuse steroids," Joe said.

"The new guys are all alike," Nathan said to Steve. "They all wear black, they're all rebels, they all have that same barbed wire tattoo. At least Jack Shine has his own identity."

"Yeah." Steve took a gulp. "He's old, he's puny, and he wears a girl's bathrobe."

Joe noticed that Dorn was listening to this with obvious enjoyment. Maybe guys like Dorn never had any real friends. Maybe this kind of stupid, arguing banter was fun for him. Maybe he was getting off pretending he was one of them, even though they were teenagers and he was in his twenties and could only get into the party with a gun. "So Joe," Dorn said, sitting up to take a long, deep drink. "Explain yourself. Why do you look up to this broken-down, old, puny, cross-dressing guy?"

"He's the only one who seems like he has a heart," Joe said.

Abruptly, all the helicopters stopped. Everyone froze. Dorn put down his beer and regripped his gun.

"They have to refuel," Francesca said. "They must have agreed to all do it at the same time." Joe was really glad she knew this stuff.

Dorn relaxed a little. "This situation is making me jumpy!" he said, guffawing. Steve laughed, too.

Must be a joke only drunks can hear, Joe thought.

"No," Tony Ong murmured into the cradle of his arms. Everyone paused and looked at him.

"Tony?" Dorn asked. "Did you . . ."

Tony's head came up slowly. "No. No. No. No, no, no, no, NO, NO NO!" As his voice got louder, he began to slap the carpet on either side of him, like a strange drumbeat. His face was twisted like a toddler trying not to cry. He threw his head back and pounded harder on the floor, using his fists, screaming at the top of his lungs. "NONONONONONO! NUH! NUH! NUH!"

Joe was more scared of this than he had ever been of Dorn.

Finally Dorn reacted. "Stop it!" He grabbed Tony and tried to cover his mouth with his free hand. The gun was poised, but tilted up safely toward the ceiling . . . for now. Tony wound from side to side like a snake, still screaming. "They'll think I'm torturing you!" Dorn cried, looking to the others for help.

You think you're not? Joe thought. But it was nerve-racking, hearing those sounds—they weren't words anymore—coming out of Tony. And Dorn was right. If the Men in Black heard this from the lawn, they might decide to chance it and storm the barricades. Joe was terrified of that possibility, even though it would mean an end to the ordeal. It would be chaos. Bullets might go in any direction. Even suspense was better than an apocalypse.

Elizabeth crawled over to Dorn, whose attempts to subdue Tony seemed to be making him more frantic.

"Here," she said, trying to put her arms around Tony. Tony was jerking like a live wire. "Stop!" she said to him. "You have to hold on."

The phone rang.

Dorn swore loudly and crawled over to it, relinquishing Tony, who curled up in Elizabeth's arms and whined softly.

"What do you want?" he shouted. "No, nothing's wrong. The beer is great. We're all drinking it. Some of the kids are doing animal impressions." He listened, frowning.

"Yeah, well, you're welcome to Ramon. Frankly, there's a couple of others I wouldn't mind sending out to you." He glared at Tony who was lying fairly still in Elizabeth's arms now. Every few seconds a big shudder would run through Tony's body. "Never you mind!" Dorn said. "Don't get greedy. Look, Sol, why don't we get down to hard negotiations? Like, what's your plan to get me out of here without me getting mad and wasting all these kids?"

Tony abruptly rolled away from Elizabeth, got on all fours, and began to scream rhythmically. Joe couldn't stand it. It was like a bird screaming. He put his hands over his ears.

"It's nothing! Nothing!" Dorn shouted over the noise. "I'm not hurting anyone! One of the little psychos is just freaking out!" As he spoke, he stabbed the gun in Elizabeth's direction, meaning, Get him quiet again!

Elizabeth tried to embrace Tony, but he stood up and started to run like a tottery one year old.

"I'll call you back!" Dorn hung up and lunged, tackling Tony at the doorway. They scuffled in the hall.

Joe drew his legs up, compressing all his muscles so he wouldn't shake. He realized that his body was pressed against Francesca's, and that Elizabeth and Nathan were squeezing in, too. It was almost an animal thing, like herding. Only Steve was left out. He was lying on his back with a beer can balanced on his chest, maybe unconscious.

They moved down the hall in thuds, Tony escaping and Dorn tackling. Shoes, elbows, and hips hit the walls: THUMP! THUMP! THUMP!

"Don't make me shoot you!" Dorn wailed. "Don't make me shoot you!"

The huddle of kids compressed even more. Arms went around necks and waists. Elizabeth was hiding her face in Joe's shoulder. They were all braced for one sound—gunshot.

There was a thud and a moan of despair from Tony. Then an eerie silence.

Joe gripped someone's hand; he didn't even know whose.

Then the front door opened and closed.

They let go of each other and exchanged stares, listening for more clues. It was quiet, then Dorn came down the hall. He appeared in the doorway, alone. "I couldn't deal with that," he said casually.

The huddle broke up slowly. "You let him go?" Joe's voice was like chalk squeaking on a blackboard. This was too much! Reckless and crazy! Reckless and crazy got you out! Doing your best to hold on, caring about people, got you more time in hell. This was not fair! Now, Tony was out there, breathing the beautiful night air. People were hugging him. . . . Joe wondered if their parents were still out there, or if they had to keep away. He had a brief, delicious fantasy of being in his mother's arms. For just a second, he wished he could grab the gun and shoot Tony for getting away.

Nathan had a different spin on it, apparently. "Thanks," he said to Dorn.

Dorn was out of breath. He slid back into his spot on the floor and popped his fourth beer. "Thanks for what?"

"You could have killed him to shut him up, but you let him go. I mean—"

"I get it," Dorn said. "Look, I'm a human being, you guys. I'm not a natural-born killer or anything. When I shot Rosen, I was . . . a little nuts. And the other two people . . . or three, whatever it was, I was desperate." He finished the beer in five big swallows. "I mean, I know I'm using you guys right now to stay alive, but I don't want to hurt any of you. Don't think I'm soft, though! If you try anything, I'll do what I have to. But do you think I want to hurt a bunch of kids? I'm just a person like you."

No, I don't think you are, Joe thought. He, for example, was feeling tremendously guilty for his thoughts a minute ago. Had he really wished Dorn had shot Tony rather than let him go free? Was he that jealous? He'd had his chance and forfeited. He shouldn't resent people who did something different. *If I live through this, I'm gonna have to make a list for confession, I've had so many evil thoughts.*

"Tony had a breakdown a while back," Nathan was telling Dorn. "He . . . obviously . . . something like this . . ."

"Yeah," Dorn said. "When I was sixteen—"

The phone rang.

"Calling to gloat!" Dorn spoke almost cheerfully. He checked his beer can for any dregs and picked up the phone. "Hey, there. You're welcome to that one." He listened for a minute. "No, it doesn't mean that. Ramon escaped and Tony was too much trouble. I like all my other hostages just fine." He grinned at the kids. Joe doubted if anyone smiled back. "No, I don't want to let the girls go! That's sexist, Sol. Now you think I'm gonna start handing you kids on a silver platter. . . . Sure I will, what do I care? . . . Yes, Elizabeth and Joe Anderson . . ." He covered the mouthpiece. "Sol wants to take inventory—Francesca Hart? That's the black girl? Okay, got her. Yep, Jericho. Steve Hennig?" He looked to the kids, who all pointed to Steve's prone body. It amazed Joe that they'd been through all this and Dorn still didn't know everybody's name. "Yeah, I've got him. Why are you asking? You've got two little informants out there. . . . No, I didn't do anything to him. He's crazy and he snapped. I'm not running a psych hospital in here. . . . I don't know, Sol. That's your department. You have to get me out of here and away from law enforcement, so I can escape. That's all I want. Why don't you guys just pull up stakes and go away for two hours? When you come back, I'll be gone and the kids'll be fine, eating Oreos and—Oh, Sol, don't talk like that! I refuse to believe that—you need to do much better than that. . . . A whole lot better. Aren't the mothers out there telling you to get their babies back? You better focus on that!" He punched the disconnect button.

"What?" Francesca asked.

"He's not being real cooperative right now." Dorn reached for another beer, then seemed to change his mind. "He said I should just give up, and since I didn't hurt any of you guys yet, he'll talk to the district attorney. Does he think I'm a moron? I've shot, like, three people! He's gonna get the charge reduced? To what? To where they'll only electrocute me twice? Does he think I don't watch TV? I could go to India and help the lepers right now and they'd still put a rope around my neck. I hate it when people think I'm stupid!"

Joe had been thinking about TV, too. On and off, all evening, he'd been trying to remember a single real hostage crisis where the guy didn't end up killing the hostages, then himself. Joe could think of lots of good plots from movies and TV shows, but on the news these things always seemed to end badly.

He also couldn't let go of his anger that Ramon and Tony were free. This was like a reverse slasher film. In those movies the weak links always bought it first. The killer would work his way through the crazy guy, the over-confident guy, the stupid guy. Slowly, all the defective kids would be weeded out, until the best kid—usually a kind-hearted, chaste girl, would ultimately get the monster and survive. That was fair. In this horror movie the more defective you were, the better your odds of survival. At this rate, Steven-the-drunk was in good position to be the next survivor.

As if he could hear Joe's thoughts, Steve rolled over and looked around, dazed. "Where's Tony?" he asked. He didn't wait for an answer, just slid back into his happy unconsciousness.

Dorn, along with everyone else, let out a tension-releasing laugh. "There's nothing I hate worse than a drunk." Dorn grinned, opening another beer.

Outside, the helicopters started up again.

"They're gonna be so mad," Francesca said. "They left to refuel and missed the whole thing with Tony."

Searchlights pierced the drapes. It was almost comforting to have them back. Steven began to snore. Joe looked at the clock on the nightstand. It was ten. *Fusion* was over. He realized he'd been harboring the idea that this ordeal would end as soon as the TV show was over. He felt like Dorothy watching the sand in the hourglass.

He wondered what it would be like to drink a beer. Steven was sleeping soundly, oblivious to all the tension. Dorn was leaning back on his elbows, sipping. It must be some tranquilizer, Joe thought. He knew Dorn would give him one if he asked, but Elizabeth would pitch a fit. Great, Joe. A guy's got a gun on you and you're scared of your sister.

He shuddered. For the millionth time tonight, he had to tell himself this was really happening. It wasn't a movie or a TV show or a wrestling match, where the outcome was programmed to make sense. This was reality, the cruelest, most random thing in the world.

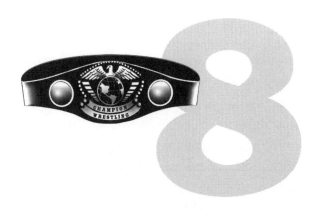

Midnight came and went. Nobody turned into a pumpkin; the FBI didn't storm the house. Some new kind of panic fluttered around in Joe's chest, like the feeling of being stuck in an elevator. A fear that maybe time would stop and they'd all sit in this bedroom together forever.

The helicopters had stopped a while ago and never started up again. Either the Men in Black had asked the press to stop filming, or they just gave up and went home for the night. Probably all the people across the country watching CNN had gotten sleepy and decided the "crisis" could wait until morning. When Joe thought of that, he wanted to punch somebody. Everyone else—the free people—could walk away from this if it got too boring, or too intense. But not them. And not Dorn. And not Solomon Page, who'd been calling a lot in the last hour, apparently trying to work on Dorn, soften him up. The two had talked from 10:30 to 10:45—a long conversation for Dorn. But then Solomon had said something that made tears come to Dorn's eyes and he disconnected and threw the handset across the room, chipping the paint on Joe's mother's closet door. Nathan had asked, but Dorn refused to tell what the conversation was about.

Steven, who'd been asleep most of the last hour, sat up now, rubbing his palms up and down his face. "Is it still happening?" he asked.

The other kids chorused, "Yes," all in the same, low-pitched monotone.

Steven shook his head, as if to throw something off. "Can I go to the bathroom?"

Dorn frowned—an impatient babysitter with too much to do—and got up. He backed around the bed, holding the gun on them and went in the bathroom that attached to the bedroom.

Joe realized what he was looking for. "It's okay. There's no window!" he called.

Steve stood up, holding the bed for support. "I need to . . ." He covered his mouth with both hands.

"Let him in the bathroom!" Elizabeth shouted at Dorn. "Before he throws up all over the floor."

Dorn got out of the way just as Steve charged. For a brief, thrilling moment, Joe hoped it was a clever ruse—Steve would disarm Dorn and end the siege, but no, he ran straight to the toilet. Dorn shook his head and closed the door, but stood beside it.

A good precedent, though, Joe thought, since he had to go himself. He was very glad Dorn wasn't going to stand over them when they went in there. He wondered if there would be any way to signal to the outside world. Yeah, right, flush the toilet in Morse Code. Like Solomon's boys were down in the sewer, checking toilet paper for notes.

But while he was thinking along those lines, an amazing thought popped into Joe's head. It was about Hurricane Clive. During the storm, they had all (including his father, because this was some years back) huddled in the master bedroom closet—the one Joe was resting his back against this very minute. He saw an image of his father reaching up, putting strapping tape around the edges of a little door in the ceiling that led to the crawl space. The crawl space!

Joe's mind began to explode like the pyrotechnics at the beginning of a wrestling match. He remembered the ant problem they had last year. Joe had followed the exterminator around, asking questions. They had been out in the garage, where there was a trapdoor in the ceiling that pulled down with a fold-out ladder. The exterminator was going up there to set foggers that would go off later, while the family was away.

"Are you going to put some in the other crawl space?" Joe had asked. "The one above my mom's bedroom?"

"It's all one space," the guy told him. "There's only a partial fire wall. I can put foggers all along the way."

All along the way. There was a passageway from this closet, that led above the back hall, above the living room ceiling, and into the garage, where the side door could be quietly unlocked and opened. This prison had a tunnel!

Steve was flushing the toilet repeatedly. Maybe he knew Morse Code. Joe tried to control his face and breathing, so Dorn wouldn't know what was going on inside him.

He could picture it. They had to wait for Dorn to fall asleep or even better, to pass out from the liquor. Quietly, they'd get in the closet—all five of them—and open the trapdoor. The closet ceiling was probably eight feet high, but Steven—if he wasn't too drunk—was tall enough to boost everybody up. Then, they could pull him up or he could climb on something—they could figure it out.

Then they would have to crawl single file through the passageway, all the way to the garage, open the other trapdoor, climb down the ladder, unlock the side door, (Joe was pretty sure he knew where the key was), and run into the arms of the Men in Black.

Steven staggered out of the bathroom looking very pale. Joe ran the whole plan over in his mind, picturing every step. How could he tell the others about it? Pass a note? Could he do that without Dorn noticing? Joe's heart pounded at the thought.

"Can I lay back down on the bed?" Steven asked. "I don't feel so good."

"Knock yourself out." Dorn sat down in his usual spot, with his back against the bedroom door, and cracked another beer. Good, Joe thought. Keep drinking.

Dorn was smiling almost fondly at Steven who curled up in the fetal position. "You eighth graders don't hold your liquor very well," he joked.

"God," Steven whispered. "Everything is like . . . spinning."

"He should eat something," said Elizabeth, maybe working on an escape plan of her own.

"No!" Steven shouted.

Everyone, including Dorn, laughed.

The telephone rang.

Dorn glared at the handset, which was near Joe. It jangled away. Joe picked it up and offered it to Dorn. Dorn frowned and took another swallow. Finally he stuck out his hand. Joe brought it over.

"What!" Dorn answered. He listened for several seconds, sipping. "I didn't like your attitude the last time, that's why. . . . No, I don't want to talk to any of them— why would I want to talk to any of them?" He propped the handset on his shoulder and spoke to the kids. "He's trying to put your parents on the phone—soften me up."

An urge to cry passed through Joe's whole body. He mocked himself, *I want my mommy.* He wondered if she'd think to tell the FBI about that crawl space so they could come in that way. Joe moved his back away from the closet door just in case.

"Oh, yeah, that's a riot," Dorn said. "Who have you got in mind? . . . Good luck finding anybody in my family who wants to talk to me." Dorn swirled the beer in his can angrily. "If you find my father, let my mother know where he is!" He made a noise like laughter, but his face wasn't laughing. "No, I don't want to talk to her either. What good is that going to do? Are you trying to make me feel bad?" He listened intently. "How about what everyone's done to me, Sol? What about that? . . . No! If you put her on, I'll hang up and I won't pick up the phone anymore. . . . NO! I don't want to—I don't care what she wants!" His voice was getting tearful again. "What are you trying to do to me, Sol?" He put the phone in his lap and took several swallows. "They've got my mom out there," he told the kids. "He wants to put her on so I'll feel bad and let you guys go."

Sounds like a plan to me.

Solomon Page called from the receiver. "Quentin? Quentin?"

"Why won't you let us talk to our parents?" Elizabeth said. "It's the least you can do."

Dorn fixed his eyes on her. "The least I can do, Liz, is not shoot you guys. I'd love to let you talk to your parents, but you're such a bunch of sneaks, you'd figure out some way to give them signals and information."

"No, we wouldn't," Nathan said. "You'd be listening. And think. It would put more pressure on the FBI to nego-tiate with you. All those moms out there, telling them to cut a deal and get us out of here. . . ."

"Shut up, Sol! You're on hold!" Dorn shouted to his

lap. "Hmmm. Jericho, you're very smart. I sure could have used you before I got myself in this mess. I think you've got a point." He picked up the handset. "Solomon? Tell my mom she can go home to my stepfather, where she really wants to be. I'll let the kids talk to their parents. But I'm going to be listening and if you try anything, I swear, I'll kill somebody. Okay? Who have you got out there? Have you got Joe's mom? Let Joe go first—he's a good kid and doesn't give me any trouble."

Joe cringed. He hated it when Dorn said stuff like that. But his hands, he noticed, were already reaching out greedily for the phone.

Dorn rolled his eyes and handed the receiver over. "Get her worked up, Joe. Tell her to tell Sol to play ball with me."

Joe took the receiver. His hand was trembling, making the receiver gently bang him in the head. "Hello?"

"Hi, Joe. It's Solomon Page from the FBI. How's everybody holding up in there?"

"Pretty good."

"He hasn't hurt any of you in any way?"

"No."

"Joe, we think it's a good sign that Dorn has let two of you escape. I don't think he's comfortable with having kids as hostages. I'm trying to get to him on an emotional level. I'm gonna put your mom on and I want you to show as much emotion as you can. Okay?"

"Yes."

"Do some acting if you think you can pull it off. I want to make Dorn feel guilty. Got it?"

"Yes."

Dorn grabbed the phone. "I thought you were putting his mother on! It sounds like you're asking him a bunch of questions!" There was a pause. Dorn blushed. He actually blushed. "Hello, Mrs. Anderson. I . . . here's your son." He passed the phone to Joe as if it were hot. "That was a dirty trick! He put her right on there!"

Joe lifted the handset. "Mom?"

"Oh, honey! Are you okay? Is Elizabeth okay?"

"Yeah, we're fine. Everyone's fine." Joe was having trouble thinking. "We saw you on TV."

"I can't believe this is happening. I should never have left you alone!" Her voice rose to a wail.

Elizabeth leaned forward, as if Joe and the phone were magnetized. Joe wasn't sure what to do. If he showed emotion, like Solomon wanted him to, he'd scare his mom.

"It's not your fault, Mom," he said.

"Listen, baby," she said. "There're a lot of FBI agents out here. They're doing everything they can to get you guys out. Mrs. Jericho is here and Mr. and Mrs. Hart and Mr. and Mrs. Hennig and . . . they've called your father."

Now Joe didn't have a choice. His throat squeezed shut. "They called Dad?"

Elizabeth made a face. "Like we don't have enough trouble. . . ."

"Honey? Is he holding a gun on you?"

"Yeah, but . . . it's a lot like Hurricane Clive. Just waiting and . . . remember the hurricane, Mom?" Maybe, maybe he could get her brain going on the same pathways as his. "Or, it's like the time we had all those ants, remember?"

"Joe, are you okay? Why are you talking about ants at a time like this?"

"I'm just remembering. All the different emergencies in this house." He couldn't say much more. "Want to talk to Elizabeth?"

Elizabeth grabbed the phone. "Oh, Mom!" Her face crumpled. "I love you, too." She sniffed several times. "I know. I know. We saw you on TV but then they cut the cable. . . ." At least she was giving Solomon what he wanted.

"Jeez," Dorn said. "This is like Chinese water torture. And we've got three more mothers to go."

"Yes, Mom. I will. I will. I won't. I . . . I love you, Mom!" Elizabeth broke into loud sobs and handed the phone back to Joe.

"Hi," Joe said.

"Oh, Joey, she's so frightened!"

"I know, but it's going to be okay, Mom. Elizabeth just feels *trapped* because we're on the wrong side of the *door*."

"Joe, you sound strange. I want you to hold on, honey."

"Sure I will."

"I'm going to put Steven's mother on now. Okay?"

"Okay . . . I . . . I love you, Mom." Joe quickly held his breath so he wouldn't cry.

"I love you, too, Joey-bear."

Joe hadn't heard that in years. He whispered, "Bye," and passed the phone to Steve. "I have to go to the bathroom," he choked out.

"Okay." Dorn, looking very subdued, followed Joe to the bathroom and closed the door behind him.

Joe turned the taps on, put the lid down, and sat crying like a baby for a full five minutes, fully aware that Dorn was listening, but unable to control himself. His brain echoed with his mother's voice. *Joey-bear, Joey-bear.*

At least he was helping with Solomon's plan.

✗ ✗ ✗

The parade of mothers and fathers took them almost until one A.M. Steve's mother figured out from his voice he'd been drinking and started scolding him, judging from Steven's sheepish responses. That provided some comic relief. Francesca's father offered to let Dorn put a message on the air in exchange for the hostages. "What do you think I am?" Dorn had cried in a rage. "Some kind of political nut?"

No, Joe had thought, just an ordinary, common nut.

Nathan went last, because they couldn't get his mother to stop crying.

"How are you doing?" he asked in a low voice. "No, Mom, don't. I'm okay. Nothing's gonna happen to me." He glanced up at Dorn. "Why did you bring Lanie and Rachel with you? You should've got somebody to watch them. They shouldn't be seeing all this with the FBI and guns and stuff. . . . No, well, yes, I'm sure everything happened fast, Mom. . . ." Nathan was starting to breathe hard, something Joe had seen many times before. "Everything happened real fast on this side of the door, too, Mom, but . . . I'm not criticizing you, Mother, I . . . don't. Don't do that, please. . . ."

✗ ✗ ✗

Nathan and Joe had been friends since kindergarten. Back then, Nathan's parents had lived in a big estate home in Eagle Trace that had been professionally decorated. Every room, according to Mrs. Jericho, was a different variation of cream, sand, and burgundy. Joe walked around Nathan's house, hearing his shoes echo on the tile floors, and felt like he was in a museum as he peered up at the antique grandfather clock or the delicate porcelain angels. Nathan's mom collected angels, expensive ones in crystal and china. In those days Joe always played at Nathan's house because all the cool toys and games were there, and because Mrs. Jericho, without really saying it directly, let it be known she worried about her son playing at the Andersons', where cookies came out of boxes instead of the oven, and where there was a crucifix on the living-room wall.

Then when Nathan was ten, Dr. Jericho had died. It was a heart attack, totally unexpected. Nathan told Joe that his mother "found a lot of things out" after that, including evidence of infidelity and worse—extremely bad money management. Once the practice was closed and the debts were paid, there wasn't much left, so the Jerichos had moved out of their elegant three-tone house into a villa in Joe's neighborhood.

Mrs. Jericho suddenly wanted to be friends with the Andersons, bribing Joe's dad with beer to come over and mow the lawn or mulch the flowerbeds. And Mrs. Jericho spent hours in the Andersons' living room, bravely ignoring the crucifix as she poured out her heart to Joe's mom, trying to avoid going to a therapist she'd have to pay.

It didn't help, though. Mrs. Jericho was on a slide into depression and now, almost four years later, she was still sliding. She worked for a while as a toll collector, and then claimed to have hurt her back and made do with her disability money. Angels, now plastic instead of porcelain, multiplied in the house like gerbils. According to Nathan his mom spent most of her day, every day, watching Turner Classic Movies and drinking Diet Coke after Diet Coke. Nowadays Nathan mostly came over to Joe's house after school.

Meanwhile Nathan took over the grocery shopping, the cooking, and most of the childcare duties of his household. Usually Nathan handled all this pretty well, but once in a while his temper would seem to flare up out of the blue, which Joe thought was exhaustion, pure and simple.

✗ ✗ ✗

"I know, Mother. It does seem like a lot of bad things happen to you. . . . This is happening to me, too. . . . That's not going to happen. Why would you even say . . . MOM DON'T SAY THAT! No . . . I'm sorry. I'm sorry. I didn't mean to yell. Just think what you . . . put yourself in my . . . I'm sorry, I'm sorry. . . . I love you. . . .Yes. Tell them I love them. Good-bye." Nathan handed the phone to Dorn and staggered over to Joe, pretending to collapse on the floor beside him. "I wonder what beer tastes like," he said.

"Don't do it," Joe said, laughing. "What did she say that made you lose it?"

"She kept repeating, 'You're going to die. I just know it.'"

"Oh, jeez!" Joe said.

Nathan closed his eyes. "She means well."

Dorn chuckled. "Don't they all?" He spoke into the phone. "Sol, that was about the most boring . . . what?"

Joe noticed that Dorn had stopped drinking beer at some point and had opened the Jack Daniels bottle. He took a long swig now as he listened.

"What's she going to say to me? That shooting people and taking hostages are bad? I already figured that out. . . . No, because I'm locked into it now, Sol. All I want is to get out of here. You need to just give me a running start. Let me have a car and don't follow me for twenty-four hours. You know, give me a fighting chance. . . . No, don't. Do not put her on! . . . Why don't you listen to what I'm telling you? . . . No, don't! Don't—" Dorn's face literally fell. All his features dropped about an inch. His eyes went dull. "Hi, Mom."

He listened for a second, his face slowly contorting into a sneer. "I don't know, Mom. What do you think?" He upended the bottle vigorously. "Give myself up—Oh, that's good. Did you get that from watching *Cops*? Explain this to me, Mommy. How come these four other mothers talked to their kids about how worried they are, and you give me movie cliches? Aren't you worried about me, Mom? You're out there. You must be able to see—what?—fifty snipers pointing their guns at me? Maybe a hundred? Did you see the ending of *Butch Cassidy and the Sundance Kid*? That's my future. And you seem pretty calm about that." Energetic drinking. "Oh, yeah, right. Listen, you probably have a date or something. . . . Oh, shut up, just shut up—" He took the receiver from his ear and held it in front of his eyes, staring in disbelief. "She hung up on me!" He looked at the kids. "That cow hung up on me! Do you believe it? In a situation like this, she thinks she can play the same stupid little GAMES!" He put the receiver on the floor and pounded it with the butt of the gun.

Joe's whole body compressed and jerked with each pound. That thing could go off by accident.

So much for Solomon's psychology training!

"Stop it!" Elizabeth shouted. "If you break the phone, none of us has a chance!"

Dorn heard her. He closed his eyes. Shudders ran through him. Slowly, he relaxed his taut muscles, clearly by some huge effort of will. Then he opened his eyes and took a long, long drink of Jack Daniels. "This is just perfect," he said softly. "I've failed at everything I ever did. Now I'm failing at this. The biggest loser in the world can walk into a post office with a gun and get his point across. Not me. Sol's not taking me seriously because two of you got out. My own mother . . . What are they trying to force me to do, guys?" His eyes pleaded with the kids. Sweat had broken out on his face.

"What do I have to do to make them know I'm serious? I'm desperate! They think I'm playing! Do I have to shoot one of you? Are they all gonna make me have to shoot one of you so they'll listen to me?"

His question hung in the air. Steve slowly rolled off the bed and lurched into the bathroom. They could hear him vomiting again.

Dorn stared at the closed door. Joe and the others stared at Dorn. Slowly, his gun arm raised, like a drawbridge, leveling the gun at the sound behind the bathroom door.

"Mr. Dorn, no!" Nathan cried. "Don't!"

Dorn shook his head as if to clear it. He took a breath. He lowered the gun slowly. Joe choked and coughed and realized he'd been holding his breath.

Dorn continued to stare at the bathroom door. Steve came out and froze, as if he sensed something. "What?"

"Nothing," said Joe.

Dorn cradled the gun in his lap. "Nothing yet," he corrected.

Around two A.M., Joe started having an imagi-nary conversation with Jack Shine. Dorn was hunched over the phone, talking to Solomon Page in a low monotone. He was halfway down the Jack Daniels bottle and looked sleepy.

Steven, having emptied his stomach twice, was ready for more beer and some food. Dorn had followed him out to the living room to retrieve the wreckage of the last pizza—apparently Steve couldn't be trusted to walk around the house loose like Joe could. Steve was sitting up on the bed, listlessly plucking pepperoni between gulps of beer.

Nathan had scanned Mrs. Anderson's bookshelf and come up with a copy of *Lost Horizon*, which he was now absorbed in.

Francesca was telling Elizabeth about a dream she had last night. Elizabeth was known to have a gift for interpreting dreams—had done it for the whole family when she was little and now offered the service free of charge to her friends.

"My job, in this factory, is to separate the poison apples from the non-poisonous apples," Francesca said, pulling her knees up and hugging them. "And I know, because I guess I've had some kind of training, that the green ones are harmless. . . ."

"Mmm-hmmm," said Elizabeth.

". . . and the red ones are poisonous. So that part is fine. But I have to pick them up with this little pair of tongs and it's hard to get a grip, you know?"

"Right," Elizabeth said.

Joe loved the way Francesca said "red." It sounded like "rhett." She was still looking beautiful, although the long evening had wilted the crispness of her lime-green outfit. He remembered the beginning of the evening as though it were a dream—his party, he and Francesca in the kitchen. He suddenly wondered if she had put on that pretty outfit for him.

Everyone's escaping, he thought, looking around the room. Dorn and Steven were drinking, Nathan was reading about Shangri-La, Francesca and Elizabeth were in the dream world. That was when the idea came to Joe to let Jack Shine walk in the door. That was how it felt: like Jack Shine was standing outside the door, waiting to help.

Joe actually looked toward the door, pictured it opening, and saw Jack Shine stride in. Instead of his wrestling costume, he wore jeans and a Gold's Gym sweatshirt like Joe had seen a lot of the wrestlers wear backstage. Fifty or not, he was still in great shape with the kind of small, flat muscles that didn't come in a bottle. Everything about him

looked cocky, from the gym bag slung over one shoulder to
the dip of blond hair over his left eye. He looked straight at
Joe, as if Dorn and the others didn't matter to him. His smile
was warm and direct, his blue eyes crinkled with amusement.
"Kid," he said. "You've got yourself in one hell of a pickle!"

Joe answered in his mind. "I know. Any suggestions?"

Shine knelt down, putting his bag on the floor, so he
could be eye to eye with Joe. His eyes weren't the grayish
kind of blue, like Joe's and Elizabeth's, but aqua, like
swimming-pool water. Like Joe's father. "Kid." Shine tossed
his head and threw a surly glance in Dorn's direction.
"I've been dealing with punks like this all my life. They
got nothin'. No guts, no brains. That punk over there, he's
got half his courage in one hand" —he pointed to the liquor
bottle "—and half in the other." He pointed to the gun. "If
you took them away, he'd cry like a baby. That's the first
thing you should realize, Joe. Every kid in this room, especially you, has more guts than that poor slob."

"I'm glad you said that," Joe said eagerly. "Because I've
kind of been wondering . . . kind of feeling like maybe I'm a
. . . coward or something."

"Coward! Look at you. You're as cool as a cucumber
with a gun in your face. What are you, twelve? Thirteen?"

"Thirteen, but, like, Ramon tried to grab the gun and
then he made a run for it. I had a chance to run and I just
stood there."

"You got it all backward, kid. It doesn't take courage to
run."

"You think I was being brave to stay?"

In his mind, Jack Shine punched his shoulder gently. "You stayed to help your sister, Joe. You stayed to protect your girl. Your buddies. You stayed because you knew they needed you. You're the bravest one here."

"I have a plan to escape," Joe said.

Francesca was still telling her dream. "Then I see that one of the red apples looks delicious, and I really want to bite it. But I know that it will poison me."

"Then what happens?" Elizabeth asked.

"I don't believe in you anymore, Sol," Dorn was saying into the phone. His words were a little slurred. "I don't believe in anything anymore. You're not gonna get me out of here. You can't. I'm gonna die before this night is over."

"He's getting dangerous, Joe," Jack Shine observed. "You guys are running out of time." He made his trademark gesture of tapping his wristwatch.

"That gun makes me feel like I can't do anything," Joe said. "Like I'm helpless."

"Never say that, Joe. Unless you've got half your body in a crocodile's mouth, I don't want to hear you say that. Remember *Rock City Revenge*? The Pay-Per-View last September?"

"My mother won't let me get Pay-Per-View," Joe said sadly.

"She won't?" Shine raised his eyebrows. "Well, anyway. El Diablo had put a Power Bomb on me and I was out! Then he went over to the nearby canyon—this was a big outdoor event—and grabbed a giant boulder and he was gonna throw it down on my chest. . . ."

"Mr. Shine?"

Shine had been gesturing wildly, acting out his story. His hands froze in midair. "What?"

"Mr. Shine, I'm your biggest fan, even if my mom won't let me get Pay-Per-View. Your biggest. I've probably sent you a hundred e-mails. But . . . well, I know the outcomes of those matches are scripted. . . ."

Shine's turquoise gaze hardened into an angry glare.

"And that boulder he had was probably made out of Styrofoam. . . ."

"You got more guts than brains, kid! Nobody talks to The Human Time Bomb that way. I oughta put you in a Figure-Four Leg Lock and see how real you think that is!"

"Mr. Shine, I need real help! That gun is real! Those bullets are real!"

✗ ✗ ✗

"How does the dream end?" Elizabeth asked.

"I bite the red apple and I start turning into a butterfly. And my parents are suddenly there screaming at me to stop, and I try not to change, but I keep changing anyway."

"Wow," said Elizabeth. "I know you like butterflies." She gestured toward the clip in Francesca's hair. "It sounds like your parents are trying to stop something good from happening to you."

"Well . . ." Francesca glanced at Joe. "They say I'm too young to go out with boys."

Dorn changed to the other ear, propping the phone on his shoulder. "I'm through talking to you, Sol. It's all over! Don't call me back. I'll call you if I feel like talking!" Dorn put the receiver down. "That'll scare him. That's all I have left. Getting to scare the FBI for fun." He paused a moment. "What are you guys doing?"

"She's telling me her dream and I'm helping her interpret it," Elizabeth said. "It's interesting. Watch. Okay, Francesca, as the dream begins you're separating apples by color. . . ."

"Oh, when you say it that way, I hear a racial thing!" Francesca said.

"Okay." Elizabeth kept her face neutral. She'd taught Joe it was very important to let the dreamer make all the interpretations.

"You know, it sounds like segregation—one color of apple is bad, the other is good."

"You mentioned boys before. Do your parents say anything to you about interracial dating?"

Francesca glanced at Joe again. "Yes. They both think it's wrong."

Joe felt his stomach jump. She had definitely glossed over that earlier. . . .

"And how do you feel about it?"

This time her eyes locked on Joe's for much too long. Joe put Jack Shine on pause. He needed his full attention for this. Elizabeth followed Francesca's gaze to Joe. Nathan put down his book. "What's going on?" he asked.

Dorn giggled. "Joe! Francesca wants to bite you!"

"Shut up!" Joe blurted, then his whole body buzzed with adrenaline as he realized his mistake.

Dorn took a pull off his bottle and set it down. "What did you say?"

"I mean . . . I'm sorry, but Francesca is a nice girl and I don't appreciate—"

"You guys like each other, don't you!" Nathan cried. "Why didn't you tell me?"

Joe tried to gesture, but his hands jerked like flippers. "We just . . . she just . . ."

"Well, well, well . . . ," Dorn said. "Still waters run deep. I like your taste, Joe. I mean, I really do. My first girlfriend was black."

"I don't like her because she's black!" Joe's voice raised again, against his will. "I just like her!"

Jack Shine interrupted. "Hey, cowboy. Watch yourself."

"Your girlfriend is real pretty, Joe." Dorn rubbed the barrel of his gun along the leg of his jeans as if to polish it. "Really, really pretty. Maybe . . ."

The phone rang. Dorn let it ring two more times, glaring at it, then answered. "Hey, Solomon. You just missed True Confession. How are things on the outside?"

Joe heard a number of exhalations, including his own.

"Saved by the bell there, pal," Shine commented.

"I know," Joe said, reverting back to speaking inside his mind. He tried to focus on Shine and ignore the fact that Steve, Nathan, and Elizabeth were all staring at him.

"Listen, Joe," Shine said. "Don't let your feelings

make you stupid, okay? The worst thing you can do is let an opponent know your weak point."

"I know." Joe tried to make eye contact with Francesca, but she'd dropped her gaze. No wonder she'd wanted to keep the whole thing a secret. He didn't think he could disobey her parents.

"Joe!" Shine said. "I feel like I'm talking to a referee here. Are you listening to me?"

"I'm sorry."

"You were right, Joe. I was trying to con you before. But let me tell you a different story. One without any boulders in it. I turned fifty last year. You probably know that, 'cause it's in all the magazines. 'How long can he wrestle?' 'When will he retire?' God, I hate reading that crap!"

"Yeah." Joe felt uncomfortable because Shine looked uncomfortable.

"You know I'm the only guy in the history of the sport that's gone this long without being turned into a 'manager' or a 'color guy'. The Bailiff is forty-four. Cardinal Crushing is forty-two. The Death Machine is forty-six and had a bypass for God's sake, but I'm the only guy over fifty, and when I hear my entrance music now? That ticking clock? I hate it, Joe. Because it's my career, ticking away, coming to an end. . . ."

"But the fans love you!" Joe protested. "Even the ones who hate you love you! When you go on vacation, the ratings go down."

"Sure, kid, but that won't go on forever. There's young guys coming up, and most of the younger fans prefer them.

They're not like you, Joe. They don't remember my glory days. They just see an old guy. You know what they've started chanting at my matches? 'Get a bra!' Look at me!" He pounded his chest. "I'm as hard as a rock, and those little creeps . . . Look, the point is, my company doesn't know what to do with me. I've done every story line known to man. Some day soon they're gonna cut me loose."

"Why are you telling me this?" Joe said.

"I'm telling you what I really know about bravery, kid. Every day, this old guy goes to the gym and works out, no matter how much it hurts. Every Friday night I walk that aisle and do my show with all those young guys who wish I would get out of their way. Year after year, day after day, I show up. I stay right there at my post whether it's a good day or a bad day, 'cause it's my duty. You get me, kid?"

✗ ✗ ✗

"My parents aren't racist!" Francesca cried suddenly, pulling her head up and looking at Joe with pleading eyes. "It's just that they both had hard lives and they want my life to be easier."

Joe put Jack Shine on pause again. "But what do you expect me to do? . . . I don't want to make you lie to them."

"You lied to me," Nathan cut in.

Joe was getting tired. Too many story lines. "I wasn't keeping anything from you. I knew I liked her but I didn't know until tonight that she liked me. She told me in the kitchen."

"You told me you liked her weeks ago," Elizabeth said.

Joe swiveled to Nathan. "She's my sister."

"I'm your best friend!"

Joe swiveled back to Elizabeth. "And I'm sorry I told you because you went and told her and then she told me and now we can't do anything about it anyway."

"Hey!" Dorn covered the receiver. "Archie and Veronica! I'm doing hostage negotiations here! Save that stuff for study hall!"

"We don't know if we're ever gonna get to study hall!" Joe shot back.

"Your temper is a problem," Jack Shine murmured.

"And you shut up, too!" Joe said. Out loud.

"Who?" Francesca, Nathan, and Elizabeth asked together.

Joe slumped. "Everybody."

✗ ✗ ✗

"What I wanted to tell you with the boulder story," Shine said with a little smile, "is that the key to survival for little guys like us is timing. You have to learn how to wait and get yourself in a good position. You've seen me in the ring: when things get rough, I go to the outside, pretend to break a lace, even act like I'm begging for mercy. That's all so I can recover and think. And when I see my shot, I deliver it with all I've got. You get me?"

"I guess so," Joe said. "Can you tell me if you think the closet thing is a good idea? Will it work?"

Shine started to say something, then changed his mind. "Gotta work your own strategy, Joe. Can't help you there. But remember this: Use everything. Wait for your best moment and deliver your hardest blow. And remember, every man has a moment of truth . . ."

"When he is tested for all he's worth," Joe finished.

Someone tapped Joe on the back. It was Nathan. "You okay, man?"

"Yeah, sure," Joe said. "Why?"

"You look zoned. I was afraid you were cracking up."

"No, I was just pretending I was somewhere else."

"Oh. Smart move. Sorry to interrupt."

"Listen. About not telling you. I don't know why I didn't. I'm sorry."

"S'okay."

"Joe?" said Elizabeth. "I'm sorry I told Francesca when you told me not to."

"No problem."

"I'm sorry, too, Joe," Francesca said. "I didn't make it clear to you how much of a problem it was."

"I didn't do anything, did I?" Steve asked the group. They all laughed.

"I'm sorry," Dorn said into the phone. "That just isn't good enough." He disconnected. He surveyed the room. "What happened?" he asked. "Did somebody die?"

Dorn was the only one who laughed.

X X X

Dorn fell asleep at 3:12 A.M. Joe listened to him breathe for a full five minutes, making sure. No one else was awake except Nathan, who was still reading his book, and Joe. Joe gently pulled the book away and put a finger to his lips. Nathan frowned, immediately seeing Joe was going to try something. Joe got up and tiptoed to the bed where Steve was snoring away. He put a very gentle hand over Steve's mouth and whispered in his ear, "Wake up and don't make any noise."

Steve flinched and his eyes flew open, but at least he made no sound. Joe whispered in his ear again. "There's another way out of this room. Follow me."

Considering all he'd had to drink, Steve caught on quickly. He eased himself up quietly, watching Dorn, who was sleeping against the bedroom door with his head tilted back and his mouth open. The gun rested in his lap with his limp hands over it. His face looked young and angelic.

Joe tiptoed to Elizabeth and whispered, "Wake up and come with me."

She opened her eyes and looked doubtful, but sat up. Joe could see them all exchanging little glances. *Does Joe have a good idea? Or is he going to get us killed?*

He went to Francesca, allowing himself the briefest of seconds to breathe in the scent of her shampoo before whispering his instructions to her. Putting his finger to his lips again, he tiptoed toward the closet and motioned for them to follow him. Elizabeth got it, but everyone else frowned at Joe and hesitated. Still, they all followed him. The weight of responsibility gave Joe a headache. What if Dorn woke up? What if this didn't work?

He opened the door and went in. The other four kids pretty much filled up the walk-in closet. Nathan closed the door, pressing it gently so the latch made the tiniest click. They all waited a second to see if Dorn was going to come storming in. Then Joe pointed to the ceiling, to the hatch that led to the crawl space. It was still disfigured with tape marks from the hurricane.

"We're going to hide?" Francesca whispered.

Joe shook his head. "It leads to the garage."

Steve's voice floated through the darkness. "He could wake up and catch us and shoot us like dogs in a trap."

Nathan whispered. "I want to go."

Joe decided to go ahead as though it were agreed. "You lift us up, Steve," he whispered. "And then we'll help you up."

Steve exhaled his protest, but lifted Joe from the waist and held him up toward the ceiling. Joe could smell the fearful sweat of everyone in that closet. The hatch was just a loose piece of wood that fit into a frame. Dislodged wrong, it would bang down on their heads. He tapped it gently, balancing it on his fingertips, easing it to the side, and it made a scraping sound. Everyone froze and waited for death.

Nothing happened. Joe scooted the hatch millimeter by millimeter, slowly revealing a doorway of darkness above them. It smelled like old, old dust and dead bugs. Joe wished to God he'd thought of a flashlight, but he hadn't. He reached his arms up and let Steve lift him higher into the unknown.

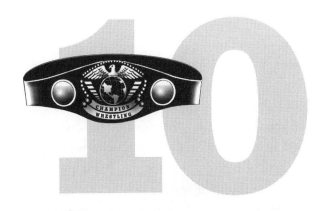

The first few seconds were awful. Until his eyes adjusted, Joe was in total darkness. He had to touch surfaces he couldn't see and pull himself up without looking clumsy in front of Francesca. Weird that such a thing would matter at a time like this, but it did. Plus he knew if he accidentally kicked anything or made a noise, he was killing himself and all his friends.

With all this on his mind, Joe felt himself lifted up by Steve. His head and shoulders plunged into pure, hot blackness. The attic had a scorchy smell, like an overheated ironing-board cover. One hand touched a splintery wood beam, sticky with dust and dirt. The other hand touched paper and a prickly cloud of insulation. Joe moved that hand to the wood and found it to be wide—something he could stand on. Feeling around, his fingers crunched into the dried out carapace of a bug. Grimacing, he re-gripped and started to pull himself up. Steve swerved and exhaled violently as dust rained down on him. Joe pulled his body up as Steve let go of his waist and braced his legs.

Leaning forward on his hands, Joe brought up one

knee, scraping his shin and picking up a splinter. Joe's eyes were beginning to adjust. He saw the plank he was holding, running like a highway to freedom in front of him. On either side of that, beams slanted down, with big sections of insulation between. The planks were paved with a layer of dead bugs. A few feet in front of him, everything was swallowed by the gloom.

Muscles trembling from the effort of moving slowly and quietly, Joe drew up his other leg. His whole body was in the attic! He rose on his knees and got to his feet, touching the beams above his head for balance. There was room for him to stand straight, but Steve and Francesca would probably have to walk hunched over.

Joe shifted his weight and the wood beneath him creaked loudly. He froze, waiting. When Dorn didn't burst into the closet with his gun blazing, Joe turned slowly, knelt, and looked out the opening at his friends. He gestured for Steve to send the next person up.

Elizabeth's blond crown appeared and began to rise, as if she were a magical being ascending through the clouds. Joe reached forward and pulled at her waistband. Her hair immediately became a nuisance, swinging around like a loose boom on a sailboat, whipping Joe's eyes and getting caught under Elizabeth's hand as she struggled.

She was the least athletic of all of them and in some ways, Joe thought, the most fearful, but she was a trooper right now. She breathed shallowly, silently working to untangle and right herself on the beam. Joe helped her stand up and gave her a quick hug.

"Let your eyes adjust and then go around me," he whispered in her ear. He prayed some quirk of the house didn't magnify that whisper and play it right into Dorn's ear, down in the bedroom.

Elizabeth nodded and stepped around Joe, using him for balance. "Stay on the wood part," Joe whispered. "I don't know what's under the insulation."

Her balance and night vision seemed better than Joe's. She was already tiptoeing away into the gloom, not even touching the ceiling, making no creaking sounds at all. Joe made a note to point this out to her if they lived long enough. She was always saying she wasn't good at physical things. She was braver than she thought, too.

Joe motioned for Francesca. Watching her rise in slow motion was like watching one of those films on Nature where a flower comes bursting out of its stem. The Goddess. Joe gripped her too tightly, swamped by feelings. He pressed his face against her soft, curly hair, and she kissed his cheek. It was the lightest, most delicate brush of lips, as she gracefully pulled her long legs up onto the beam.

Maybe if I save her life, her parents will reconsider.

Joe helped Francesca step around him, resisting the urge to grab a quick grope.

"You girls start walking," Joe whispered. "We want to get as many people out as we can in case . . ." He decided not to finish that.

Francesca nodded, but hesitated. She reached up, pulled the butterfly clip out of her hair, pushed it into the pocket of Joe's cutoffs, which almost made him fall right off the beam. Then she turned and vanished into the shadows.

Nathan. Joe tried not to let memories flood into his mind—the backyard campouts, the games of beach Frisbee with Nathan's dog, the time when they were twelve and managed to drive Nathan's mom's car halfway down the block before smashing into a mailbox . . .

Joe grabbed at his friend a little roughly, suddenly aware of how much time was going by. Until they were all safely hidden in the attic, they were as vulnerable as wounded animals in a trap. Joe and Nathan had climbed trees together. It was comfortable and easy for them to do this maneuver. "Don't expect *me* to kiss you!" Nathan whispered as Joe hoisted him up.

"If we ever get out of here, I just might."

Nathan was agile and stepped around Joe easily.

Joe prayed they didn't sound like a herd of elephants to the rooms below. They must not, or Dorn would be in there by now. Thank God the guy was a drunk. Joe knew how soundly they could sleep.

The next thought made his heart flip-flop. What if Solomon chose right now to ring the telephone? Dorn would wake up, see them gone, search the house. . . . No, his back was to the bedroom door. He would know they were in the closet.

"Come on!" he whispered to Steve.

Steve jumped high enough to grasp the floor of the attic. He adjusted his grip and then executed a pull-up of the kind Joe could only dream about. "Grab me," he rasped.

Joe reached over Steve's back, grabbed him and pulled, while Steve writhed his way forward like an alligator. This was by far the noisiest thing they had done. As soon as Steve was all the way in the attic, he flipped himself around and replaced the piece of wood over the opening.

Joe felt immediately safer. He started to walk, Steve lumbering behind him, creaking more than anyone else, huffing and puffing, too.

Joe stopped and let Steve bump into him. "Shhhh," he whispered.

"It's so hot," Steve whispered back.

"Next time we're in a life and death thing, don't drink so much beer!" Joe hissed at him. Then he felt guilty. Maybe Jack Shine was right about his temper.

"Sorry," Steve said softly.

Joe walked slowly, putting each foot down carefully, both to maintain balance and to try to avoid the inevitable creaks and squeaks. He could see only a few feet ahead, where Nathan's lean body was a shifting shadow that sometimes disappeared. Looking down, Joe could see the beam he walked on, only about a foot wide, and the word "Corning" stamped on the slabs of insulation. The air was hot and stifling. Every three steps or so, he would crunch a dead bug.

He wondered where he was in relation to the house. Over the living room? Halfway to the garage? Or maybe they were all still in the master bedroom, right above Dorn's head. Maybe Dorn had heard them and was aiming his gun at the ceiling right now. . . . Joe's steps faltered and he grabbed the beam above his head for balance. This was the time to move mechanically and quit thinking so much. *Every man has his moment of truth.*

Nathan had vanished up ahead. Joe walked a little faster. He looked down and saw a weird object in front of him on the beam—a small statue or figure. At first he thought it was a little barn owl. Then he thought it might be one of the foggers the exterminator had put there last year. As he got closer, he realized it was a little doll of some kind.

Unable to resist, he stooped and picked up the toy. It was a Batman action figure, complete with swirling cape and tiny utility belt, fuzzy with old dust. Neither Joe nor Elizabeth had ever had such a thing. The previous owners of the house must have had a kid who ventured up into this crawl space one day to play with his Batman. Something about that made Joe very sad. He almost pocketed it, but decided to leave it as a kind of house guardian. Behind him, Steve paused to look at the doll too, and then moved on. It almost felt like a ritual.

How big is this house anyway? It was nerve-racking. Joe kept visualizing that trapdoor in the garage. They would come to the air-conditioning unit first, then the ladder folded up on the floor, over the hatch. It was important to visualize each step, force the images into reality.

Ahead, Nathan was stepping over something. Fire wall, Joe thought. Thank God it didn't go all the way to the comb of the roof.

There was a muffled sneeze up ahead. Joe froze and Steven bumped into him again.

"Shoot!" Joe whispered.

"Think of another word," Steve whispered back.

Joe felt a kind of pressure building up in his stomach. This was all taking too long, giving Dorn too much time to wake up and figure things out. Joe's mind was going haywire from the swirl of doubts and fearful thoughts he couldn't control.

Before he saw the air conditioner, he heard its hum growing louder and louder. Joe's optimism surged back. *We're really getting out of here!*

Greedily, Joe remembered the feel of night air—freedom air! He could feel the strength of the Men in Black pulling him to safety, like they had done with Ramon. He could see his mother in her writing-class outfit, holding out one arm to each of her twins.

Now he saw the shadowy forms of Nathan and Francesca standing by the air-conditioning unit, looking down with great concentration to where Elizabeth was already descending the ladder! Joe hurried the rest of the way. He was just in time to see the gleam of her blond hair sinking into the darkness of the garage below, like a jewel falling into deep water.

Francesca and Nathan went next. Joe moved up greedily. He could hear the echoes of the girls' whispers below. Joe's heart pounded. The freedom air was only minutes away!

Steve put his big paw on Joe's shoulder.

"After you," Joe whispered.

"After you," Steven said with a sweep of his hand.

So Joe got on the ladder. The muscles in his calves

trembled so hard he could barely climb. A sudden sweat broke out on his body. He felt someone touch his back to encourage him as he stepped off the ladder.

Then the garage light came on.

All of them gasped, except Elizabeth, who screamed outright. Dorn stood there, leaning against the wall like he'd been there for a while, pointing the gun right at them. His eyes were pale and stony.

Joe stepped back from the ladder, fighting a powerful urge to cry. How could Dorn have been that smart?

Dorn snapped out of his slumped position like a snake and stepped forward, gesturing with the gun for Joe to get away from the ladder.

"Run the other way!" Joe screamed up the ladder.

Dorn went into fast motion and Joe's mind went blank. He was grabbed by the collar and jerked violently away from the ladder, his body banging into Dorn's like a tethered balloon. "I ought to KILL you," Dorn growled as he slammed Joe into the garage floor. Joe's left cheekbone felt like a hammer had hit it. He lay very still, afraid to move or open his eyes.

Dorn, meanwhile, was shouting up the ladder to Steve. "Come on down! Don't be stupid!"

Apparently Steve preferred Joe's advice, because he could hear the loud pound of sneakers on the ceiling.

Dorn let out a long stream of curses. He grabbed Joe's collar and hauled him up, choking him. "You did this!" he shouted. "You betrayed me! I trusted you!"

He whirled on the others, huddled by the garage door.

"Get away from there! Get in the house or I'll splash Joe all over you!"

It was lucky most of Joe's air was being cut off by his T-shirt collar or he would have laughed hysterically—definitely the wrong thing to do. No one else was laughing. They bolted like a pack of deer for the door into the kitchen. Dorn followed, dragging Joe with him. Joe tripped and fell over the threshold, his collar cutting even deeper into his throat. He wondered if he could accidentally die this way, when Dorn wasn't even trying to kill him. He scrambled, banging his shins, until he was on his feet again and could breathe.

Inside the house they could hear Steve's footsteps clearly, explaining how Dorn had been able to track them. "Get on the couch, and if you move, Joe's dead!" Dorn said to the others. Joe was turned the wrong way, so he couldn't see if they cooperated, but they must have, because Dorn turned his attention back to the ceiling. "I can hear where you are! You hear me? I can shoot right up through the ceiling and kill you!"

The sound of footsteps immediately stopped. Joe noticed there was something wrong with his eyesight. He closed his right eye and saw that he was looking through a narrow, letterbox opening on the left side. The whole left side of his face must be swollen.

"I know where you are, Steve! I'm right underneath you, hear me? I'll shoot right up into your valuables! You want that? Go back to the closet and come out slowly or you're dead! It's all over! Joe's little plan didn't work."

Even though he knew it was wrong, Joe blurted out, "Why do you think I planned it?"

Big mistake. Dorn shook him like a bad dog and growled in his ear again. "Because it's your house! Because I know your type! You were PLAYING me, being so nice and cooperative, weren't you, Joe? Weren't you, Joe?"

Joe's brain and body were too rattled to do anything but go limp. Meanwhile, Steve had started moving again, doubling back toward the garage.

Dorn paced along with him, still dragging Joe like a toddler drags a teddy bear. Dorn's sweat had a sharp smell, like horses after they've been running.

"Knock it off!" he screamed at the ceiling. "You go back the other way! Or I'll shoot you and everybody else!"

The footsteps went back toward the center of the living room. Joe thought of a runner caught between the bases. Why didn't Steve just give up? Didn't he realize he was killing them all? "I'M NOT PLAYING!" Dorn shrieked, but the footsteps went faster. Dorn lunged, trying to stay under Steve and Joe got smashed into a chair.

Steve doubled back again, toward the garage, feet pounding the beam. Then there was a muffled thud and a sound like a big sheet of ice cracking. Joe looked up.

For a split second there was the surreal image of thousands of little cracks breaking out in the ceiling above them, like someone drawing a spiderweb on the other side. Steve screamed, and Dorn and Joe both instinctively knelt and hunched over. The cracking sounds were thunderous, like a million branches breaking, and then the ceiling rained down—plaster, dust and Steve.

Everybody was screaming. Chunks of debris hit Joe's back. Dust poured on to his head. Something sharp cut his arm. When Joe looked up through a fog of plaster dust, he saw the front door open and close.

Dorn recovered and lunged at the door, trying to juggle his gun into firing position, but Steve was gone. Steve was free. Joe licked his lips and tasted blood and gypsum. Dorn stared at the door. His hair was white with plaster dust. All around him, it snowed.

Dorn slowly lowered the gun. He looked at Joe, still lying in the pile of rubble. Then he looked at the kids on the couch. "Did you see that?" Dorn asked. "Did that really happen?"

Joe had the same feeling. But it must have happened. He could look up and see the massive hole in his ceiling, looking like a burst-open baked potato. A strip of pink insulation hung down like a party banner. He could shake his head and shoulders and see little chunks of plaster and bursts of dust fly off. He could see there were only four of them now, alone with a guy who was now ten times more crazy and frustrated than when he came in.

And then Joe almost gave in to that hysterical laughter again—there was that little Batman figure on the floor, just inches away. Steve must have slipped on it. That was why he fell. Right to his freedom. Joe palmed it, shoving it into his pocket beside Francesca's hair clip.

Clumsy. Add that to the list of important survival traits. You could be reckless like Ramon, or crazy like Tony, or drunk and clumsy like Steve.

But if you were smart or careful or thoughtful, you would end up like Joe: covered in dust, one eye swollen shut, a shoulder pounding with pain, and blood coming from somewhere you hadn't even figured out, yet decorating the plaster all around you. You could be the focus, as Joe now was, of that wolf-stare. Dorn was just standing at the door, staring at Joe, his gun hand hanging down at his side. Staring.

"You did this," he chanted quietly. "You're like all the other ones I've known, but you're the worst, Joe. Look what you've done to me. Look what kind of FOOL you've made out of me. But I'll tell you this." His voice was almost musical, running up and down a scale. "You're going to be the last. You know that, Joe? You're going to be the last."

The telephone rang back in the bedroom. Joe was very relieved, because he was pretty sure if it hadn't, Dorn was planning to wring his neck.

Dorn stared down the hall in the direction of the sound. He seemed to be listening to the ringing as if it contained messages he could interpret. A little piece of plaster slid out of his hair and made a puff of dust on the carpet.

Abruptly, he grabbed Joe by the collar again and strode off toward the bedroom. Dorn found the phone on the bedroom floor. "You're calling at a bad time!" he said to Solomon. Without breaking stride, he dragged Joe back to the living room, where the other three were still huddled on the couch. Joe was really glad all three of them hadn't headed for the door.

He wondered if it was because they were loyal to him, or because they didn't think they had enough time.

Dorn let go of Joe's T-shirt and Joe fell, rolling onto his back. Dorn gently but firmly planted a foot on Joe's chest. "No, I don't think that's going to happen," he said into the phone. "I don't think we want any more of that type of thing. Joe's not in my good graces right now." The pressure on Joe's chest increased, just a little. Dorn aimed the gun at Joe's face and pretended he was sighting down the barrel. He squeezed one eye shut and contemplated different angles, like a photographer. "That's tough. I bet you worked really hard on that. Any luck finding my father?" He laughed, but it sounded awful, like the scream of a hawk. "I thought not. . . . No. Joe has lost his telephone privileges. He's been helping you all along, hasn't he, Sol? Giving you signals, helping those other guys to get out. He probably planned the whole thing, to have that big ox kid fall out of the ceiling on me. I'm not as stupid as you think." He pressed the disconnect button and took his foot off Joe's chest. "Let's go in the kitchen, children. I don't like having you this close to the front door."

The kids on the couch stood up in a nervous clump. Joe was afraid to stand up so close to Dorn.

"Don't piss me off!" Dorn grabbed his collar again and hauled him up. Joe coughed as Dorn shoved him toward the saloon-style doors, giving him a kick to propel him through them. Joe landed on his already sore, bruised face.

Joe could hear Elizabeth breathing hard, but for once she didn't pop off. This wasn't reassuring. It meant she saw something new and scary in Dorn's behavior.

The other kids came over to Joe, who was pulling himself

up off the floor. "Can we put a wet paper towel on his face or something?" Francesca asked.

Joe wondered what his face looked like. He swiveled around to look at himself in the black, glass oven door.

"Hey!" Dorn actually cocked the gun. "What are you doing?"

Joe put both his hands out. "I'm not doing anything. I'm not planning to do anything."

Francesca sat down on the floor next to Joe, apparently too scared to wet a paper towel without permission. Elizabeth sat on his other side and Nathan on the other side of her.

Dorn smirked. "Here's something different to occupy your little mind. Guess who Solomon had on the line from Flint, Michigan?"

Joe's stomach did a flip, and he grabbed Elizabeth's hand. "Our father? Our father was on the phone?"

Dorn nodded, smiling sadistically. "Hallowed be his name."

Joe's heart pounded. He didn't know what he was feeling, but something big and powerful. It was like the feeling when the roller coaster plummets, or when lightning hits the ground really close to you, or when you startle a flock of birds and they fly right at your face.

Elizabeth shook her hand free of Joe's. "We don't want to talk to him anyway."

Joe's unstable feeling galvanized into pure rage. "What did you say?" He turned to her so violently, she pulled back into Nathan.

"I'm sorry! I don't want to talk to him." Her face was smudged with dirt from the attic. She had a black streak across the bridge of her nose.

Joe wanted to hit her. "How can you? . . ." the words jammed up for a second. "This might be the last night of your life, you stupid—"

She leaned into his face now. "Don't you ever talk to me that way!" she hissed. "You're just like him sometimes!"

Joe wasn't even sure how bad this insult was—was she comparing Joe to their father or to Dorn?

"Hey! Hey! Hey!" Dorn waved the gun. "Order in the court! The hostages aren't allowed to kill each other!" He laughed again, the same horrible hawk cry.

At that moment Joe didn't care about Dorn. He was so furious with Elizabeth, he wanted to grab her and smash her head against something. Then he was even madder because a thought like that proved her point. The blood pounded in the sore part of his face. There were too many confusing signals in his brain. He struggled to get to what was important.

"Please call Solomon back," he said to Dorn. "Please let me talk to my father."

Elizabeth turned her face away from him.

"Please," Joe said. "Please let me talk to him!"

He felt Nathan's hand on his back. Some kind of caution or warning, but Joe didn't care.

Dorn's smile had gotten bigger and bigger as Joe begged. "Everything that goes around comes around, doesn't it, Joe? You spend the whole night screwing me over and betraying me. . . ."

"No, I didn't!" Joe pleaded. "I swear I didn't."

". . . make me sick," Elizabeth whispered beside him.

"You be quiet!" Francesca said to Elizabeth. Everyone, including Dorn, looked at her with surprise.

"You mind your own business!" Elizabeth hissed back at her. Joe was nervous for a minute, being between them. They were glaring at each other, muscles tensed. But Elizabeth shifted her anger back to Joe. "What's wrong with you? How come you go out of your way to make bad people like you? What are you trying to do?"

Joe suddenly felt close to tears. He guessed that was what Nathan was warning him about. Lots of times Nathan could see Joe was losing control long before Joe could see it. "I just want to talk to my father!" Joe wailed. His voice sounded about six years old.

"What's your definition of bad people, Liz?" Dorn asked in a funny voice. "Men?"

She met his eyes fearlessly. "Pretty much!"

Dorn chuckled. "Don't worry, honey. With your attitude, they won't bother you too much, anyway. So, Joe. Let's talk. How much do you want to talk to your father?"

Nathan's hand was back, firmer. What was his deal? "A lot," Joe said, and abruptly, his throat closed and the tears started pouring out of him. "Oh, God!" Joe choked, totally caught off guard. He couldn't stop it, either. It was like a volcano erupting. His diaphragm spasmed, and sobs, big and loud, tore out of his mouth. All three of his friends were touching him, including Elizabeth, who had her head down. Then she looked up at Dorn. "Are you happy now?"

Joe couldn't see how Dorn reacted to this because he was blinded by tears. There was no sound in the whole kitchen but his own noises—gulping, gasping, whimpering. God, it was so humiliating.

Finally, Dorn spoke. "Knock it off, Joe," he said. "I get your point."

Joe struggled, but it was like the hiccups. He couldn't break the cycle.

"Knock it OFF, Joe! If you want to talk to your father, go ahead. Jeez!"

Joe clenched both fists and forced himself to take a long, deep breath. His body shuddered. He was so ashamed, like a little kid who wets his pants in school. You'd never see Jack Shine doing a thing like this! "I'm sorry!" he gasped. "I'm okay. I just . . ."

"I'm sorry, Joe," Elizabeth said. "I didn't realize how you feel about Daddy."

Joe shrugged, but he felt angry with her. How could she not know? Where was the famous twinsight now?

✗ ✗ ✗

Joe remembered how alone he had felt the day his father left, standing in the front hall, paralyzed. He was unable to go toward the kitchen where he could hear his mom and Elizabeth talking quietly. He was unable to go back to the master bedroom where his father was packing. In the end he ran out the front door.

He plowed down the street like a power walker, trying to burn off all his angry energy. Two doors down, there was Nathan, sitting in his front yard, playing with his sheepdog. "What's the matter?" he called out.

Joe knew he couldn't walk on by; Nathan would run after him. Why hadn't he gone the other way? He slowed his steps and tried to put on a neutral face.

"What is it?" Nathan asked.

"Nothing." Joe stooped to pet the dog. "Hey, Lex, how you doing?"

"You have a real funny look on your face," Nathan said cautiously.

Joe shrugged. "Know what I saw on the internet yesterday?" He threw Lex's fetch ball and watched him run.

Nathan smirked. "Does it involve girls?"

Joe pushed him. "I read that Jack Shine's contract is up and that he might really retire this time—he's been having back problems. So maybe that 'I Quit' match on the next Pay-Per-View is real."

Nathan threw the ball this time. "You're nuts. They plant that stuff to sell tickets. Jack Shine will never retire."

"He will someday." Joe realized his voice sounded strained. "I don't know what I'll do. . . ."

Nathan lobbed the ball high. Lex leaped after it like a shaggy dolphin. "There're ten thousand other guys on the roster, Joe. You'll just pick one of them to be obsessed with."

"But . . ." Joe heard the car start up in his driveway. Something happened in his body that made him feel like all the bones had locked at the joints.

Nathan kept his attention focused on the dog. "I heard your dad . . . come home last night."

Joe couldn't move. He stared at Nathan's lawn, watching it blur through his tears. He could hear the car backing down the driveway.

Nathan pulled his dog into a hug, burying his face in the fur. "This was supposed to be his last chance, right?"

"Right," Joe whispered. The car engine was fading now, as it rolled off down the street.

"And I guess this time she means it," Nathan continued.

Joe nodded. Now there was no sound at all.

Nathan's voice was soft, gentle. "Maybe he'll get the help he needs and—"

"No!" Joe was through with fantasies like that.

Lex was squirming in Nathan's arms. He let go. The neighborhood was so quiet, you could hear the birds singing their heads off in the trees.

Nathan put his hand on Joe's shoulder. "Jack Shine will never retire," he said.

X X X

The phone rang in Dorn's hand. He answered it immediately, keeping his eyes on Joe, like he was the crazy one. "Yeah? Yeah, I know. We're discussing it now." He pressed the handset against his shirt. "They've still got him on the line, Joe. What do you want to do? I won't put you through any more crap about it."

Joe didn't know what to do now. What if he started crying again? He sure didn't want to do that in front of his dad. It felt like all the will had been sucked out of him. It didn't matter if he ever talked to his father again. It didn't matter if Dorn shot him. Joe had failed and failed and failed and cried. He was worthless.

"I don't know."

"Hold on," Dorn said into the phone, and then put it back to his chest. "Come on, Joe. Talk to him. At least *your* father called."

Joe glanced up at Dorn, who looked like a vulnerable kid. How could this be a triple murderer? This guy was exactly like Joe. He just wished his father cared about him more. It wasn't a reassuring thought at all. It made Joe think that any one of them might end up where Dorn was right now. Joe held out his hand for the phone. He took a deep breath. "Hello?"

"Hi, Joe, it's Solomon. How you doing, my man?"

Joe sniffed. "Okay, I guess."

"Gets pretty rough when this stuff goes on for hours. Remember, the bad guy is getting as worn down as you. We're gonna get you out of there, Joe. You gotta hang on."

Joe realized this speech was a response to his post-crying voice. Even the FBI was patronizing him. "I know," he said.

"We reached your dad in Flint, and he's waiting to talk to you and Elizabeth. Okay?"

Joe wiped his face on his shirt. "Okay."

The line cracked and then there was the voice of Joe Senior. "Joey?"

Joe waited a second. He wasn't going to cry again.

"Joe? Can you hear me?"

"Hi, Dad." A weird-sounding attempt at a bright tone.

"I've been talking to Mom. You know there's a whole bunch of special agents and stuff working on this. They're gonna get you out and then we're gonna fix that creep but good! I'll see to it personally that he fries."

Joe looked at Dorn, who was using his fingers to comb plaster out of his hair. He realized his father and everyone else in the world who had never been involved in something like this, didn't have a clue what it was really like. "You bet!" he said.

"Your mom's holding up pretty good."

"Good." This wasn't the conversation Joe wanted at all. Come to Florida and rescue me. Say you're sorry you left. Promise to stay with us forever.

His father's voice probed cautiously. "How's Lizzie?"

"She's okay." Good thing she hadn't heard him use the name she hated. Joe remembered how his father never got anything right. Never. *You're just like him sometimes.*

"Could you put her on, sport?"

Joe looked at Elizabeth, using his twinsight to transmit. She shook her head no. Her eyes looked undecided, though.

"I guess she doesn't want to," Joe said. He glanced at Dorn who had stopped combing and was following this with interest.

"Aw, no. Really? I mean, I know she's mad at me, but at a time like this?"

"I don't know. That's what she says."

"Even your mother is talking to me! What's the matter with her? I'm her father!"

"I know," Joe said. "But . . ." Elizabeth was looking at him questioningly, asking for an update. Joe covered the receiver. "He really wants to talk to you."

Elizabeth hesitated, then held out her hand. "Hello?" she said, like she didn't know who was calling. "Yes. Yes, we're all right. . . . I know, yes. . . . What do you mean?" She glanced at Joe. "I'm not! I just . . . this isn't the best forum for having a talk, that's all. Have you talked to Mom?" This was said very pointedly. Joe looked at Dorn again. He was gazing at them, like Joe's family story was the best soap opera he'd ever seen.

"I didn't say that, Dad." Elizabeth's cheeks were flushed. "Oh, no! I'm sure you are! You must be feeling all kinds of things. . . . I think you know what I mean! . . . Well, it's pretty obvious. Maybe if you'd been here, this never would have happened!"

Joe was badly jolted by that statement. He could imagine how much it must have hurt his father. After living with

Elizabeth and Mom, Joe sometimes wondered if he could ever stand to be married to a woman. They could be so . . . brutal.

Either their dad was doing a lot of talking or none at all, because Elizabeth was silent for several seconds. "Dad?" she said finally. "Look, I didn't mean that. We're all so exhausted and scared. . . . Yes. I can't lie about that. I'm very angry with you. I thought you knew that."

"This is not the time. . . ." Joe said.

Elizabeth gestured for him to be quiet. "What? . . . I don't want to hear about that right now. I kind of have enough . . . what?" She closed her eyes as if enduring a terrible pain. "Yes, I know that. I know you do. I . . ." She looked up at Joe like a helpless little kid. Tears brimmed in her eyes. "I do, too, Daddy." She thrust the phone at Joe.

"Dad?" Joe looked at Dorn again. He was staring at Elizabeth.

"Hi, sport. Wow. Your sister really knows how to sucker punch, doesn't she? Just like her mother."

"I don't know." Joe was losing his temper. "Can we talk about that someday when there's not a guy holding a gun on me?"

"I know, I know. I guess both of you are in a pretty agitated state."

"I guess!" Joe said. If he wasn't so mad he would have laughed at that statement. Francesca pulled Elizabeth into her arms. Elizabeth was crying quietly. Dorn's eyes went unfocused.

"Joe?" said his father. "You there?"

"Yeah."

"Joe, what she said about my not being there. You don't feel like that, do you?"

"Nooooo . . ." Joe wondered what he did feel.

"Your mother made me leave. I didn't want to. You guys both know that."

"That's the way I understand it." Joe was getting furious. Did it always have to be about him? Even now?

"If I could be there right now, exchange places with you . . . I'd like to kill that lousy punk. . . ." His father broke into muffled sobs.

If anything, that made Joe angrier. "I know. Elizabeth was just . . . we just wish a lot of this had never happened. That's what she was trying to say."

"Alcoholism is a disease, Joe."

"Yes, I know. I saw the brochure. Could we talk about that after the hostage crisis?"

A long pause. "You're angry with me, too."

Joe gave in. "Yes."

"I can't believe it! At a time like this!"

"Exactly, Dad! At a time like this, I don't want to be talking about you! This particular moment, Dad, is about Elizabeth and me!"

"Yes!" Dorn shouted so unexpectedly that everybody jumped. He was staring at Joe with eyes that were so intense, they seemed to glitter.

"I'm sorry, Joe," said his father. "I'm obviously saying

the wrong things. I'm sorry. I'm always sorry. I'm always wrong. I love you guys and I hope you'll forgive me for everything wrong I did in the past and whatever I'm doing wrong now and everything wrong I'm gonna do in the future!" The line clicked and crackled with static. Joe couldn't believe it.

"Joe?"

"Hi, Solomon. I guess my father hung up on me."

"He what?"

"We got into some family stuff and he hung up on me."

Solomon's voice ran up an octave. "At a time like this?"

"Yeah." *Will you be my father?*

"Well, now I've heard everything. I gotta tell you, I didn't expect that."

"Well, our family is pretty special," Joe said.

"Not really!" Dorn said.

"I'm sorry, Joe. I really am. I sure don't want to add to your stress. I gotta say, your mother warned me, but I thought she was just talking like a divorced woman."

"He's not a terrible person," Joe said wearily. He and Elizabeth looked at each other. "He does the best he can."

"You think?" Solomon said. "Listen. Tell me about that crawl space you kids tried to use. It's accessible through the garage?"

"Yes."

Dorn took the phone. He must have seen a ray of hope in Joe's face. "Okay, Sol, you're not his dad. Are we all done with your morale session? Because honestly, it brought all of us down. You better file that technique under 'Worthless.' My mother hung up on me, Joe's father hung up on him. Liz is here crying. . . . You're supposed to wear me down, not my hostages!" He giggled. "No, no, don't start with that stuff. . . . No. You've seen all the escapees you're going to see. I'm not letting them get out. It's easier to hold a gun on four kids. It would be even better if I could shoot one and just have three. It's late and I'm tired and I want to get out of here. So quit horsing around with the phone calls and get me a helicopter or something!"

Dorn hung up the phone. His face had been animated when he talked to Solomon, but now the life seemed to drain away. After a minute, he said in a low voice, "What are we going to do, guys? I don't know how to end this story. I don't think he can really get me out of here, so what am I doing? I think we're all dead. I think we're all dead and just waiting for the gun to make it official. What's the point? Does anybody out there really care about us? Maybe we should just do something to show them." He wasn't really looking at anybody, he was just staring into space, reciting his words. "We're all alike, really. There's no difference between you guys and me. Kids and criminals. People just want them out of the way. We should show them, Joe." His eyes suddenly woke up and focused on Joe, who jumped. "We should show them. What if they all came in here and

we were just laying here like Jonestown? Then—"
He stopped as if a plug had been pulled in his brain.

He stood up, still looking at Joe.

A low whine came out of someone's throat. It was the last thing Joe heard before he blacked out.

Joe woke up, flat on his back, in the middle of a wrestling ring. The squared circle. Bright lights shone in his eyes from somewhere in the ceiling. The area beyond the ring was pitch black. Jack Shine, wearing a blue singlet, boots, and knee pads, was perched on the top rope. In the brilliant light, he looked like something cast in gold.

"I hope this isn't Heaven," Joe said, sitting up.

"Nah!" Shine hopped down and leaned back into the ropes, as if he were going to slingshot himself. "You passed out and I thought I'd take the opportunity to give you a little coaching, pal. Time's running out and you need to find a finishing move."

"That's easy for you to say!" Joe shot back. "You're not in a room with a gun in your face!"

Shine used the ropes to swing himself back and forth. "We're all in some kind of room with some kind of gun, Joe. But you're a born hero. If anybody's gonna save the day, it's gonna be you."

"You're nuts!" Joe said. "Hero? Did you see my so-called escape attempt? Did you see me on the phone with my father? Crying like a baby?"

"Your so-called escape attempt got one more kid out. Your crying weakened your opponent. Everything you've done tonight has weakened him. That's exactly how you win a match. You work and work and work on a guy's weak point, and when you know he's got nothing left, you come in with your best move." He demonstrated, clamping his Moment of Truth Sleeper Hold on an imaginary opponent. Then he dropped to the canvas and slapped it with his hand. "One! Two! Three! Ding-ding-ding!" He jumped up again and raised his own hand. "Best feeling in the world, Joe. Dorn hasn't got much left. He's staggering around on his last resources. But instead of planning your pin, you're focusing on all your mistakes, Joe. What you don't realize is, he's doing the same." He counted on his fingers. "First mistake—he killed a bunch of people and ruined his life. Second mistake—he went to the wrong house—yours—and got trapped like a rat by the FBI. Third—he really sucks as a hostage taker, Joe. You're supposed to, at the minimum, keep the hostages with you, not let them run out the door. Fourth—and take it from me, Joe, this is the big one—he's done all that and he still can't get his parents' attention. And your little talk with your daddy drove that point home for him. He's a loser, Joe, and he knows it. A jobber. He's self-destructing. Your job is to make damn sure he doesn't take you and your posse with him."

Some of this actually made sense. "Okay, I agree with you that Dorn's a loser. But would you mind telling me what I ever did to make you think I'm a born hero? Because that point is escaping me right now."

Shine chuckled. "You picked me for your hero, kid." He polished his knuckles on his chest. "Heroes pick heroes for their heroes. You know who Dorn admires? Kurt Cobain. You do the math."

"I don't know who that is," Joe said.

Shine exhaled impatiently. "You young kids just get younger all the time. Band called Nirvana. Drugs. Premature death. It's a common story. We've got a few kids in our business that went down the same road. Anyway, that's what your gunman thinks is glamorous. Screwing up and dying young."

"Well, I'm glad you're so sure about all this," Joe said. "Could you please tell me how I'm supposed to finish him off? Considering he has a gun?"

"Everybody has to come up with their own moves, Joe. That's like your signature. I can't give you my stuff. Just do what I've been telling you all along. Weaken him, use whatever you have against him, watch your timing, and when you know he's as weak as he can be, go in with something big and pin the sucker."

Joe sighed. "I guess it's asking too much to hope for the FBI to do this instead of me."

Shine shrugged. "Hope all you want, kid. Hope for your parents to get back together. Hope for your father to be less selfish. Hope your mother will be more forgiving.

Hope that your sister will quit popping off at an armed gunman. You can waste your whole life, kid, hoping everybody else will give you what you need. Or you can lace up your boots and go take it for yourself."

The sound of a telephone bell shattered the dark silence beyond the ring.

"Oops," said Shine. "There's the bell." He winked at Joe. "Gotta go."

"Wait!" Joe yelled, but the ring dissolved, and he was lying on his mother's bed with a pounding headache and a very sore face. The phone was ringing. Norman Bates came into focus, surrounded by his stuffed birds. WE ALL GO A LITTLE MAD, SOMETIMES. Joe sat up and saw Nathan, Francesca, and Elizabeth sitting on the floor, all looking at Dorn in terror. Joe followed their sight line, and his body jolted at the sight of Dorn sitting on the floor by the bedroom door, holding Mrs. Anderson's stuffed gorilla in his arms. His eyes were big and lost looking, like a kid separated from his parents in a department store.

"Aren't you going to answer that?" Nathan said to him.

Dorn stared at him and shook his head no. He hugged the gorilla tighter.

"Do you want one of us to answer it?" Francesca asked.

For an answer, Dorn raised the handgun and pointed it directly at the phone.

"Okay! Okay!" Joe said. "Don't do that."

The phone rang two more times and quit.

Dorn rested his head on the gorilla's shoulder. Joe and his friends exchanged looks.

"I must have passed out," Joe said, glancing at Dorn.

"You did," Elizabeth said. "We—Mr. Dorn—"

"Charlie!" Dorn said suddenly.

"What?" said Elizabeth.

"Charlie." Dorn nuzzled the gorilla's fake fur.

"He's asking you to call him that," Joe said to Elizabeth. "Quentin Charles Dorn. I guess your friends call you Charlie, right?"

"Friends!" Dorn said bitterly. "Ha!"

Elizabeth blinked several times. "Okay, so anyway, Charlie carried you in here and put you on the bed and then he was talking about how rude Dad was to hang up on you and then he started to say some things about his dad. . . ."

"Oh, no!" Dorn wailed.

Francesca finished the story. "And then he got real *nervous*, like he is now."

"I knew this would happen," Dorn said. "I knew this would happen. I knew this would happen."

"Charlie?" Joe said.

Dorn looked up with exaggerated hope.

"I want to ask you a sort of . . . unusual question. Did you ever . . . were you ever a fan of the band Nirvana?"

"Oh, God!" Dorn nodded his head rapidly. "It was just so sad, you know? Like how a genius like that can just . . . can just . . . can just . . ." He shrugged and slowly leaned back against the gorilla.

"What did you ask him that for?" Elizabeth said.

"Never mind," said Joe. "But if we get out of here okay, I'm going to start going back to church."

✗ ✗ ✗

The phone rang. Joe glanced at his mother's bedside clock. Four-thirty A.M. Through the crack in the drapes, the sky still looked dark. Joe fingered the souvenirs in his pocket: the little Batman action figure, Francesca's butterfly clip. He wondered if daylight would change things. Almost anything would be better than this. Almost. His face still throbbed, and he was so tired now his spine ached. He felt itchy and dirty from the attic.

Strangely, no one had fallen asleep again. The other kids were slumped, and Dorn was in a very odd position. His butt was on the floor, and his torso was leaning over on the gorilla—half sitting, half reclining. But his eyes were wide awake. And his grip on the gun still looked strong and firm. Joe understood he was weakened. Jack Shine was right about that. But if anything, that made him seem more dangerous. Joe certainly couldn't understand how he was supposed to "work on him" or come up with a "finishing move."

The ringing phone, which Dorn ignored, made Joe angry. Was that all they knew how to do? Sit out there all night and make phone calls? Solomon Page was a pretty poor negotiator in Joe's opinion. All he'd done was change a relatively stable gunman into a lunatic, monkey-hugging gunman. Couldn't they just chance it and come in? They knew about the garage, the passageway. Wasn't their name Special Response? It was a pretty weak response so far.

Joe thought about his dream or hallucination or whatever it was. Weaken him. Use whatever you have. . . .

"Can I answer that, Charlie?" he asked.

Dorn looked up, eager at hearing his name. Then he frowned. "N-n-n-n-no . . ."

"Please? It's driving me nuts."

Dorn laughed. He had a new laugh now, high-pitched and giggly, like a girl. He slowly raised the gun and aimed it at Joe with both hands. "Bang, bang, bang," he giggled. "Go ahead. You're dead."

Only fifty percent sure Dorn wasn't really going to shoot, but almost too tired to care, Joe crawled off the bed and picked up the phone. He noticed his friends were frozen and looked really scared. Strangely, Joe felt fairly calm. Maybe he had given up all hope.

"Hello?"

"Joe? What's happening? Why haven't you been answering in there?"

His concerned tone struck Joe as ludicrous. "Yes, we have plenty of food left. We have nuts and bananas and some assorted flakes. . . ."

"Dorn's cracking up? Are you in immediate danger?"

Joe looked at Dorn who was pointing the gun at himself, peering down the barrel. "I don't think so. But we'll have to run out of food eventually."

"If we made a move, would he react? Is he capable of shooting erratically?"

The gun was aimed at the gorilla. "You take that back!" Dorn giggled.

"Yes," Joe said to Solomon. "Most definitely, yes."

"What's he saying?" Dorn asked Joe, looking suddenly lucid.

"He wants to know if you want anything special to eat," Joe improvised. "Or some more Jack Daniels, maybe . . ."

"No more deliveries!" Dorn cried imperiously. He leaned over and whispered to the gorilla. "That's how people get away."

"We have even more nuts than I thought we did," Joe said.

"Don't panic, Joe. I know this is really upsetting, but we have to go slowly and carefully. So far nobody's been hurt, and I don't want to make a rash move and mess up that nice record. So, ask him what he wants. I need to get him where he's negotiating with me again. Tell him he can have anything. I don't want him to give up hope."

Joe thought that moment had already passed, but Solomon was the expert. "Solomon wants to know what you want."

Solomon whispered into the phone. "Tell him he's won. I'll do anything to make him happy."

"He says you've won. He gives up. He'll give you anything you want."

Dorn lay on his back. "Tell him to fly around the world like Superman and turn back time." He spun his index finger in a slow circle.

Joe took a chance. "Cut that out. Come on, be serious, Charlie. That's the least you can do. You owe it to us to try to get us out of here alive. He's telling you you can have whatever you want. Come on. Think of the possibilities."

"Good," Solomon whispered.

Dorn sat up. Tears stood in his eyes. "I'm sorry, Joe. I'm sorry. But he can't do anything. If he says they won't grab me and put me in jail, he's lying. There's nothing he can do. It's over. It's so over."

Apparently Solomon had heard that. "Damn. Still, if he can still think that clearly he's not totally out to lunch. Joe? You've been with him all this time. Is there some angle? Can you think of anything that might work?"

Use everything you have. "Charlie? What if Solomon could get your father to call?"

"Good, Joe," Solomon whispered.

Dorn jumped or flinched, like a current had run through him. "They won't even be able to find him."

"They're the FBI, Charlie. If they want to find the man, they'll find him. And if they tell him to get on the phone, he'll have to get on the phone."

Dorn laughed. "Yeah. Boy, that would be funny. They'll chase him down in his little rat hole and point their guns at his face for a change and they'll say, 'You get on the phone, Mr. Dorn!'"

Okay, Jack. I found his weak point and I'm gonna hammer it. "He's the one who ought to be in all this trouble anyway, not you!" Joe said. "He's the bad guy!"

"Oh!" Dorn said looking deadly serious. "He's much worse than you think. Would they hold a gun on him and make him get on the phone and listen to anything I want to say to him?"

"Would you hold a gun on Mr. Dorn senior and make him listen to everything Charlie has to say?"

"We'll cuff him and mace him, if necessary," Sol said. "Now get him to say that he'll let you walk free. It's important to get him to acknowledge his contract."

"Okay. Charlie? They can do it. But you have to promise if you get to talk to your father—"

"And say everything I want, and he can't hang up like my mom and your dad did."

"Right. He'll stay on the line, and you say whatever you want, and he has to listen, but then you'll let us out. . . ."

"And give yourself up," Solomon prompted.

"And give yourself up."

"Give myself up . . ." Dorn turned to the gorilla as if seeking advice. "I don't know."

"Charlie, listen to me. They're gonna get you anyway. You knew that since ten o'clock," Joe spoke with desperate earnestness. "You just said you know they're going to put you in jail. If you keep holding us, or if you hurt us, they're just going to prosecute you worse. But at least, if you hold out for this one thing and then let us go, you'll get the satisfaction—"

Dorn put his hands over his ears. "No, I can't give up. They'll lock me away."

He's on the ropes. Hammer him. "It's gonna happen anyway, Charlie. This way you get something!"

Dorn took his hands off his ears and stared at Joe. He looked punch-drunk.

"All you can do now," Joe said quietly, "is take your dad down with you."

"He's watching this on TV right now," Dorn said. "Thinking like, 'Ha, ha, not my problem.' But I can make it his problem. I can shove it down his throat that this is his problem. Then this . . . all this will mean something, won't it, Joe?"

"Yes!" Joe said, hearing the other kids echo him. "That's it, Charlie. You can make a statement for all the kids everywhere whose parents don't pay attention."

"Yes," Dorn nodded up and down vigorously. "Yes."

"But you have to agree," Joe said patiently. "You have to agree. The deal is, you talk to your father, he listens to whatever you care to say, and we go free. Saying the word "free" sent shivers of joy through Joe's bloodstream. His friends were all leaning forward, hopeful again. Joe prayed he was finally on the right track.

"And record it. I want it recorded, so the news will play it."

Joe wanted to scream from frustration, but he held it in.

"Solomon, he wants the conversation recorded, so the news will play it and everybody will understand what he stood for."

"Of course. Whatever he wants. But make him say his part of the deal."

"Okay," Joe said. "You can have all that if you promise to give yourself up when the phone call is over and let us go free."

Dorn looked almost like his old self. He leaned back against the bedroom door. "Tell him it's a deal."

"Deal," Joe exhaled the word.

"Great. Tell him we need a little time to track his father, but Joe, I promise you, we'll get this thing done. In the meantime, it's your job to keep him as calm and as happy as you can."

"Okay . . . Charlie? We'll have to give them some time to find your father, but then it's all gonna happen, just the way you want."

"This is all destiny," Dorn said to the ceiling. "We're all part of a big . . . destiny."

"Yeah . . . ," Joe said. "I'm hanging up now, Solomon. Please work fast."

"You have my word." The phone disconnected.

Dorn was still nodding to himself. Joe got the feeling he was hearing words in his head and agreeing with them. He wondered if this would work, if they really had time before Dorn just gave up and started emptying rounds for kicks. Still, for the first time that night, Joe felt he was playing a game he was good at, doing moves he felt more sure of.

"Because now he'll know something about me," Dorn said as if they had heard the internal part of his conversation. "And I want to tell him something about himself, too. I'm really gonna do him a big favor because he's walking around not knowing what a son of a bitch he is. But after tonight, he'll know. And if they lock me up or even if they kill me—he can't say he had nothing to do with it."

"Right," Joe said.

"I know you and Elizabeth understand," Dorn said. "I'll bet you'd give anything to get your old man in a vise and let him have it."

"Yes, I would," Elizabeth said. "The first thing I'd want to know is how dare he hang up on Joe when we're in a situation like this!"

"Yeah," Joe said softly. "All he wanted to talk about was the divorce and him being an alcoholic and his stuff. And *I'm* the hostage for God's sake."

"Right!" Dorn said. "Right!"

"I have really good parents," Francesca said softly. "But I wish they wouldn't expect miracles all the time from me. Like if I get an A, they say, 'Of course you did.' But that means they don't appreciate how hard I worked and how. . . scared I was till I got the A."

Dorn looked wide awake at this point.

Joe realized they would have to play group therapy until that phone rang again. "Nathan? What would you have said to your dad if you could?"

Nathan laughed. "Please don't die and leave me to take care of your family! But it wouldn't have worked. Parents never listen."

Dorn's eyes looked so soft, they were almost human. "No. They never do."

"Why is it taking so long?" Dorn asked the ceil-ing. "What time is it, Joe?"

Perspiration ran down the sides of Dorn's face, even though the room wasn't hot. His beard was starting to come in, shadowing his cheeks and chin. Repeated finger combings had disheveled his wavy hair. His upraised, agonized eyes reminded Joe of the statues in church.

"Five-fifteen," Joe said. The sky still looked black through that tiny gap in the drapes, but a bird outside was singing. Joe couldn't imagine it. The whole house surrounded by guys with rifles, and this stupid bird was sitting in his usual tree, singing his usual song.

"Maybe he killed himself," Dorn said. "Maybe he decided he'd rather die than talk to me."

Joe realized Dorn was talking about his father. "It hasn't even been an hour yet. They just haven't found him. It takes a while to track people down."

His Christ-like head lowered, the pale eyes leveled at Joe. "Not for the FBI."

Francesca spoke up. "Things take longer to set up than you think. My father—"

"Screw your father!" Dorn told her. "I've heard enough about your father. It sounds like you're one of the Cosby kids or something. Just keep it to yourself."

"Who?" she asked.

Dorn turned away from her, back to his favorite friend, Joe. *Lucky, lucky me.* "I'll tell you what's going on. He just doesn't want to do it. The bastard doesn't want to do it! They're probably saying, 'Mr. Dorn, we'll slap you in the pen for three hundred years if you refuse to cooperate.' And he's going, 'Anything's better than talking to my worthless son!'"

"No," Joe said in the tone he used to lure stray dogs. "You have to—"

"I DON'T HAVE TO DO ANYTHING!" Dorn screamed. He smacked the carpet in front of him. "I'M THE ONE WITH THE GUN. WHY DOESN'T ANYBODY REALIZE THAT?"

"We realize it!" Nathan said. "Believe me!"

Joe knew they had to get him distracted again. "Tell Elizabeth one of your dreams," he said. "She's amazing."

Dorn laughed. "I don't think you little kids can handle the kind of dreams I have."

Outside there was a weird noise, a slow whooshing. Joe realized it was the helicopters starting up again. *Good morning, CNN, we're still here.*

Dorn stared in the direction of the sound. Then he turned back to Elizabeth. "What's the point in shrinking me now, Dr. Liz? It's much too late for rehabilitation."

She shrugged. "It's just something to do. You enjoyed it when we did it before. Why shouldn't you take your turn?"

"Why, indeed . . ." He stared at the wall again, listening to the helicopters, rising and making their slow passes over the roof. "I'll tell you a dream," he said. "But please, Liz. Don't get your hopes up. Bigger and better shrinks than you have tried to figure me out and they all throw up their hands."

"I'm not going to figure you out," Elizabeth said. "No one can tell you what your dreams mean. You have to listen and decide for yourself."

Dorn looked interested. "Okay." He raked his hands through his hair again. "Okay. Okay. This is the dream. I'm a little boy in this dream, like five or six, but I still know I'm me. You know?"

"Mmm-hmm," Elizabeth said.

"I'm walking through a . . . not a cornfield, but some kind of farm . . . a ploughed field. Like they've ploughed up the dirt, but nothing's growing yet. Those little hills. Do you know what I mean?"

"Furrows," Joe said.

"Yes! Furrows. But it's a huge field. The rows go on forever, all the way to the horizon. And the sun is hot, it's beating down on me and it's dusty. I always have this thought—I won't make it out of this field! I'm going to die!"

"That's upsetting!" Elizabeth said.

Boy is it! Joe had felt a jolt when he heard it. He didn't have a lot of nightmares himself. Nothing about death or dying had ever come into his dreams.

Dorn was sweating again. He seemed to sweat from his temples, the drops running down the sides of his face like tears. "Somehow I know in the dream that if I could make it to the end of the field, I'd survive. But I can't. It's hopeless. Every step gets slower and my legs hurt and the air gets thicker and dustier and the sun gets hotter and closer. . . ." He swayed a little. "And I lay down, staring at the sun, and I feel myself dying. . . ."

"What does that feel like?" Joe asked, even though he didn't want to know.

"Like water draining out of something. Like . . . like something going down the drain."

The room was silent. The helicopters roared and receded, roared and receded.

Elizabeth finally spoke. Her voice cracked. "Is that the end of the dream?"

"No." Dorn shook his head. "No, I wish it was. I'm laying there, dead, like paralyzed with death, but I'm still in my body and I can still see. Not like those nice TV shows, where you slip out of your body and fly around. I'm stuck in a dead body forever—awake but dead! And I . . ." He looked down. A drop of water fell from his face.

"Is that the end of the dream?" Now, Elizabeth was begging.

Dorn closed his eyes, squeezing them. He shook his head. "Then the ravens come," he whispered.

Joe wished to God Steve was still here. Because right at this point he'd say "Caw-caw" or "Nevermore" or something, and force everybody to laugh and break the tension that was building up all around them. But the jokers and crazies and hotheads all go free in this world. Only the good people have to stay and hear about the ravens.

"Big, black ravens . . ." Dorn's eyes turned up so suddenly that Joe actually glanced at the ceiling to see if the ravens were there. But of course, they were only there for Dorn.

". . . circling in the sky above me. First one, then two, then six, then a whole flock of them . . ." His arm described slow circles above his head. The helicopters added eerie background music. "Wheeling around . . ."

"That's what they would do," Nathan said quietly. "Over a . . . carcass. They make a flying display to show a . . . food source to other ravens."

"Ravens eat dead people?" Francesca's face was twisted with revulsion. "I thought that was buzzards."

"Ravens, too," Nathan said.

"You know a lot about birds?" Dorn asked him.

Nathan blushed. Even in a group of nerds, this was a nerdy hobby. "Yeah," he mumbled.

Dorn nodded. "I do, too. But not these . . . tell them, Nathan. Tell them how big a raven is."

Still blushing, Nathan cleared his throat. "Around two feet long, including the tail. Head, like the size of a cat's." He demonstrated the skull by putting two hands together.

"Yuck!" Francesca said.

"Yes!" Dorn seemed delighted that his dream was grossing them out. "They're really big and they fly over me. I can hear the beating of their wings and they get closer, and closer, and then they start to dive, pull up, dive again, getting so close and staring at me—are their eyes brown, Nathan?"

"Yes."

"I've seen their eyes! And they're looking at my eyes, and I know what they're going to do. They're going to peck out my eyes!" Dorn's voice rose to a wail.

"Oh, stop!" Francesca turned away and covered her face. "Don't tell us anymore!"

Joe realized he had both hands over his mouth, as if to hold in a scream. "God!" he said.

Dorn nodded rapidly. "I know. It's horrible. That's when I wake up, just as they get close to my eyes and I realize that's what they want. I guess that scares me enough, and I wake up with a feeling like ginger ale all over my body!"

"God!" Joe said again. It felt good to shout out something, like it could push the images from his mind.

"How long have you been having this dream?" Elizabeth asked. She still looked perfectly calm, but Joe knew that she was shaking on the inside.

"Do you know a lot about ravens?" Nathan asked. "Because your dream was really accurate. Like, the aerial display . . . and the part about the eyes . . ."

"Jeez!" Francesca covered her face with her hands.

Nathan ignored her, eager to share bird lore. "Because if they find a carcass that hasn't been torn open by a predator, they can't . . . well . . . they can't open it for themselves, so they take the only part they can get out easily. . . ."

"The eyes!" Dorn said. "I wonder how I knew that?"

"Jung says the unconscious mind knows all kinds of things like that," Elizabeth said.

"I was supposed to read him for a class," Dorn said. "I couldn't get through it. You little brats really are geniuses, aren't you?"

If we were, we'd have the gun by now.

Elizabeth was revved up by the acknowledgment of her intelligence. "The important thing isn't the symbols themselves. It's the feelings you had in the dream. I guess it's pretty obvious, but how did you feel in that dream?"

"Doomed." Dorn said it casually. "And then, sad, when I knew I was dying. And then really, really scared, because it was like . . . even dying isn't the worst thing—there might be something even more horrible. . . ."

"What feels like that in your waking life?" Elizabeth asked.

The telephone rang. Everyone jumped.

Dorn smiled. "My father."

The phone rang again. It sawed on Joe's nerves. "You want me to get it?" he asked Dorn.

Dorn shook his head no. He held his shaking hand over the phone for several seconds as if trying to bless it, while the bell drove little spikes into Joe's nervous system. Finally, finally, Dorn picked up the handset and pressed the button. "Yes?" A pause. "Oh, hi, Sol. Oh, yes, we're still having fun. Are you having fun out there?" He winked at the kids. Then he frowned. "Uh-huh. Seattle. How about that! And . . . oh, wow! Let me . . . hold on, I want to repeat that to the kids." He covered the mouthpiece.

"They've got him on the line from Seattle. I'm surprised they got a phone line to run under a rock! Anyway, this is what Sol just said to me. 'He understands the importance of the situation and wants to speak to you.'"

Yeah, okay, you're real important. We get it.

"Talk to him," Elizabeth prompted.

Dorn uncovered the mouthpiece. "Put him on! Hello . . . Yes, it's me. . . . Yes, I can hear you. So, Dad, do you understand the importance of the situation I'm in here?" He chuckled and listened for a while. "Oh, yes, I certainly do understand that." He covered the mouthpiece again. "He's telling me he'd never speak to me voluntarily, just because people's lives are at stake." He spoke into the phone again. "Right, Dad. Now I hope you understand my perspective. I have to threaten innocent children just to get the things normal people expect. You see . . . Yes, I'm admitting I'm not normal. I'm *your* son, right?" Dorn laughed, but it sounded forced. "Oh, don't go down that old road, Daddy. I'm yours all right. I guess you just don't want to believe that you're the father of such a disturbed individual, right? 'Cause it's all genetics, you know. Crazy begets crazy. I think Freud said that on a real bad day. . . . What crap? I think I was making a very interesting point. . . . Oh, now you're giving me orders! That's funny, Dad. 'Cause I have the gun. Boy! Think what you'll look like if you upset me and all these kids die. The FBI won't be happy with you! CNN will say, 'Mr. Dorn, why couldn't you have said a word of compassion to your troubled son just to save the helpless children,' and then you'll have to say something like, 'I looked into my tiny heart and I just didn't have any compassion. Sorry about the kids, though!' . . . Oh, I apologize. I was trying to entertain you. See, I've never found the right things to say to you. If this isn't working, wow! I'm fresh out of ideas!"

Joe started to wonder if this whole conversation was a good idea.

"What?" Dorn asked his father. "What do I want? Did somebody hand you a card with that written on it? . . . Okay, you're right. I do want something. I want the chance to remind you of what a god-awful father you were to me." He listened for several seconds. "Aw, that's sweet." He covered the mouthpiece. "He says he knows he made mistakes." Back into the phone. "Know what they were? Can you list them? . . . BEEEEEP! Time's up. Sorry. Thank you for playing. Sit back, Dad, and relax. Ready? Okay!" Dorn got to his feet. The situation was energizing him, making him all peppy and strange. Joe didn't know if it was a good thing at all. Dorn started pacing up and down in front of the bedroom door, stepping over his friend the gorilla.

"Item number one—Christmas, when I was nine years old. Where were you? Mom said you were out helping Santa Claus. I think you were out with Jack Daniels. Item number two . . ."

Joe wondered if this stuff was going out live on CNN. The edges of the drapes were bright red now. The sun was rising.

"Item number two, throwing a book at Mom and hitting her in the head. . . . Yes, you did. . . . Yes, you did. You're just supposed to listen. This is a big list, I don't have time for your rebuttals. Item number three, almost beating me to death with an extension cord the time I was sick and threw up on your new couch. Item number four, murdering my pet rabbit . . . Yes, you did. . . .Yes, you did. Okay, how did he die? . . . Let the record show the phone line went silent." He glanced at the kids, who were apparently the jury. "Items, let's say five through twenty—miscellaneous beatings you gave me and Mom, separately and in combination. Item number twenty-one—leaving us, although that might count in your favor. Item-number twenty-two—what? . . . I told you it was a long list. . . . Do I?" He covered the mouth-piece. "He says I have an overactive imagination. He loves to say that." Back to the phone, pacing and pacing in the small space, throwing his hair out of his eyes like a nervous colt. "You're right, Dad. I do. Right now I'm imagining four kids with their brains blown out, and it's all your fault. . . ." Abruptly, he swung around and aimed the gun down at Nathan. Everyone gasped. Slowly, Nathan raised two shaky hands and held them in front of his face, as if he hoped they could stop a bullet.

Joe felt some kind of brand-new anger, different from all the previous angers of the night. Maybe he was just tired and it was easier to let go, but it felt like there was a new reason to be angry. A better reason than when Dorn was a stranger. This was an anger Joe had no desire to conceal or hold down.

They could hear the tone of Dorn's father's voice now, loud and pleading.

"What do I want?" Dorn asked. "That's a much better attitude. Let's see, what do I want from you?"

Suddenly, it was clear to Joe. It was cheating again. Dorn was cheating. Just like bad wrestlers cheated. Just like Tony had cheated by having a breakdown. Just like Ramon had cheated by risking his life and running for the door. Just like Steve had cheated by turning his own clumsiness into an attack.

"I want you to say you're sorry," Dorn said. "For every lousy thing you ever did to us, you worthless, drunken . . . that's what. You say, 'Charlie? I'm sorry you had such a miserable dad.'"

It was cheating because . . . because Joe wanted that kind of apology from *his* father! But since Joe was too decent to hold a gun on any innocent people, he'd never hear it. Never. Everyone was getting things Joe wanted—the things he needed—and it WASN'T FAIR.

Dorn was listening. "Thank you," he said and hung up. He sat down on the carpet. "It wasn't very sincere," he reported. "But I made him do it. I made that bastard crawl."

Like the wrestlers who took steroids instead of learning moves. Like people who get athletic scholarships to colleges when they don't care anything about college. Like when girls say a guy is cute and they really just mean he's tall. Like when your mother and father say they're always going to put you first . . .

"So now you have to let us go, right?" Nathan said quietly.

"Huh?" Dorn said.

"That was the deal." Nathan's voice rose to a whine.

"He listened. You said what you wanted to. You got your apology. You said if you got all that, you'd let us go."

Dorn blinked. "I don't think I said that!"

"Yes, you did!" everyone chorused.

Except Joe. No one had noticed, but he was panting now, flooded with some kind of energy, some *power*. His heart was growing huge in his chest, beating, beating.

Unfair! Unfair! Unfair!

The phone rang.

Dorn picked it up, looking a little confused. "Hello? Oh, hi, Sol. That was great. Made my day. You might want to look into his tax records, too, by the way. What? . . . No, I didn't. . . . No I didn't. . . . I wouldn't have said that. . . . I'm not going out there and let you throw me down in the dirt like those guys on COPS. Well, if I said that I guess I lied."

UNFAIR! UNFAIR! UNFAIR!

"Well, I'm sorry, I just—" Dorn stopped and looked up with startled eyes as some kind of weird locomotion propelled Joe across the room. Joe saw his own hands clamp on Dorn's gun wrist. The barrel of the gun pointed right at Joe, but all he did was wrestle and squeeze that wrist, because Dorn was going to put that gun down whether Joe had to die in the process or not.

Focus on the gun. Nothing else matters. You
have to get it out of his hand before it can hurt you. That was
the object of the game, which might have been simple,
except for the voices of fear screaming in Joe's head like a
thousand pterodactyls.

For a few seconds Joe had the advantage. It was a
swerve Dorn hadn't expected. In fact he almost let go of
the gun when Joe grabbed his hand, but then Dorn
regripped the revolver and growled at Joe. Now Dorn had
the advantage—the rage of betrayal.

Joe was kneeling on Dorn's lap and dug his knee into
Dorn's groin as hard as he could, using both hands to
strangle and shake Dorn's right hand, as if it were a
stubborn chicken that wouldn't die. To keep his advantage,
Joe chanted through his teeth, "Cheater, cheater, cheater."

He faintly heard his friends screaming along with the
pterodactyls and then he felt a sharp blow to the back of his
head. Idiot! _You left him with a free hand!_

Joe wasn't sure if the voice in his head was his own
or Jack Shine's. He let go of Dorn's hand and rolled to

the side, wondering if he was about to die.

KEEP GOING! This time it was unmistakably Jack Shine's voice. *Don't give up! Countermove!*

Joe figured if he was dead anyway, he might as well die fighting. Continuing with his roll, he brought one foot up and connected hard with Dorn's jaw. Dorn screamed in surprise and let go of the gun. Joe immediately batted it so it slid under his mother's bed. Peripherally, he saw Nathan dive in that direction.

Keep attacking! Keep him off balance! He's bigger than you!

Still on his back, Joe tried to kick again, but Dorn grabbed his foot. His face was all bugged out and red. He snarled and reached for the other foot.

Don't look at his face! Use your hands! If he gets you by the feet, use your hands!

Joe dug his hand into his pocket and found the Batman action figure. He pulled it out and stabbed right into Dorn's eyes.

Dorn gave a scream of his own and Joe felt both his ankles released. He pulled his legs under him and came up in a kneeling position. Dorn had covered his face with both hands.

Disable him now! While he can't see you!

Joe threw his whole weight on Dorn, knocking him on his back, splaying and pinning his arms. Dorn's head banged against the bedroom door. Remembering to keep his weight high on Dorn's body, he planted his knees on Dorn's ribcage, so all his weight was on the bigger man's center of gravity.

Vaguely, he heard Nathan yell to someone, "Help me!"
There must be some trouble getting the gun. The bed was
heavy and low to the ground. Maybe the gun was out of
Nathan's reach.

*Don't worry about them, worry about you. He's much big-
ger than you. In a minute, he'll figure out how to kick out of
your hold. You have to know what you're going to do next.*

Dorn didn't know wrestling fundamentals, that was for
sure. At the moment, he was clearly astonished that a
smaller person was holding him down. He did the wrong
thing, struggling with his arms and upper body, making
himself tired, wasting energy on his anger. "I'll kill you,
you little . . ." He was growling.

Where was the gun?

*Don't count on anybody else. You have to do this yourself.
How can you disable his legs?*

Joe wished Jack Shine would provide a few answers
instead of just asking questions. But then he had an idea.

"Somebody!" Joe screamed over his shoulder. "Tip the
dresser over on his legs!"

"No!" Dorn shrieked and instinctively started kicking,
which was the last thing Joe wanted. The way out of the
hold was to raise your legs up and slam them down, which
would effectively throw Joe off.

"Hurry!" Joe said. Dorn had the technique and was trying
to perfect it. He bucked violently under Joe, but Joe held
on. He could hear scuffling and shuffling behind him.

"Don't clear it off, just knock it over with everything on
it!" he screamed.

"Look out!" Francesca screamed, and the dresser fell, smashing Dorn's lower body and creating a breeze behind Joe. Something hard hit him in the back of the head and several objects bounced off his back. Dorn gave an agonized scream, making Joe wonder just where the edge of the dresser had fallen.

Nathan and Francesca, who had apparently been the dresser tippers, jumped on Dorn now, adding their weight. They had to disable him completely, since he was blocking the doorway. Dorn's struggles were futile, but he kept it up.

It was like trying to hold down a hysterical dolphin.

"We can't get the gun," Nathan panted, repositioning himself up on Dorn's shoulder. He knew wrestling fundamentals as well as Joe. "It's way under the middle of the bed. Even Elizabeth can't scoot under far enough to reach it. And we can't move it, either. It weighs a ton."

"I've almost got it," Elizabeth called in a strained voice. "I can touch it, but not . . ."

"Get something to bat at it with!" Joe said, wondering why he had the only clear head in the room.

"I'll murder you!" Dorn interjected. "You have to let go sometime."

"Where's the phone?" Nathan asked. "If we can't get the gun . . ."

"I don't see it," said Francesca. She got off Dorn and crawled around. "I think the dresser fell on it."

"Leave it," Nathan said. "Just get the gun!"

"Like you babies would even know how to use it!"

Dorn taunted. Taunting was all he had left at the moment.

"You probably don't know how to use it either!" Nathan shot back.

Keep thinking! Jack Shine's voice intruded again. *Don't count on the gun if it's not here now. Always have backups on your backups.*

"Francesca, go get something to tie up his hands," Joe said. "There's a bathrobe hanging behind the bathroom door."

Dorn bucked again. He groaned in frustration, then focused a slit-eyed look on Joe. "You just think you're Superman right now, don't you, you little jerk? Just wait till I get loose. I'll tie you up and kill you so slowly, your friends'll get bored watching it!"

Don't think about that! Focus on what you need to do!

Francesca appeared with the bathrobe sash. Joe wondered what in the heck Elizabeth was doing. She'd had time to take the bed apart by now.

"Okay, wait," Joe said. "We don't want to rush this. We have to move his arms up, but keep them perfectly straight. If he bends his elbows, he has leverage."

"Right," Nathan agreed.

Carefully, he and Nathan began to edge Dorn's splayed arms up, so they could tie them above his head. Dorn fought them every inch of the way, hissing, "Little bastards!" and other choice phrases.

"When we get his arms together," Joe said to Francesca, "you lash them together, just as tight as you can, okay?"

The sash was trembling in her hands. "Okay."

Joe suddenly had a brilliant idea. "Elizabeth! Forget the

gun! Just open the window and yell at them! Tell them we've got him down!"

No! Don't panic him, Joe!

But the advice came too late. Dorn's eyes showed white all around the pupil and his whole body, suddenly ten times stronger than it had been before, bucked and jackknifed. He got his left arm loose from Nathan and slammed it into the side of Joe's head. The next clear image was that Dorn was loose and sitting up and shoving the dresser off his legs.

Francesca tried to open the bedroom door, but Dorn's body blocked it. He made a grab for her leg. She threw the bathrobe sash over his head and pulled it tight around his neck. Now Joe knew he loved her.

But it still wasn't enough. Dorn managed to reach up and pull her hair. She tried to hold on through the pain, but he was pulling her off-balance, too. The sash went slack and he had the dresser off and he was up.

Oh, God.

Dorn made straight for the window, where Elizabeth was struggling with their mother's intricate system of window locks, grabbed her around the waist and threw her all the way over the bed, where she crashed into Joe.

It's happening too fast. I can't think what to do!

Meanwhile, Francesca had gotten up and was trying to open the bedroom door. Before she could do it, Dorn bounded across the room and threw himself against the door, which she had just opened a few inches. It slammed shut.

He's not watching you. Go get the gun. You need to get the upper hand.

Joe slithered toward the bed as unobtrusively as he could, trying not to hear that Dorn was apparently slamming Francesca repeatedly against the door. He peered under the bed and managed to locate, dead center, the faint gleam of the gun. He reached. Couldn't get it. He tried to slide into the narrow space. It was tight, but he could do it. For once it was good to be the smallest. He wriggled in further, till his fingers brushed the metal. This was as far as Elizabeth got, but Joe had a feeling he could go further, since he had narrower hips. He wriggled again and his fingers closed over the prize. Before he could even be happy, he felt a hot, rough hand close over his ankle.

Don't panic, kid. You have the gun. You can make him let go now.

Joe wasn't sure, though. He wasn't gripping the gun correctly; his fingers were wrapped around the barrel and Dorn was dragging him out. He tried to flip the gun around in his hand, terrified he was going to accidentally hit the trigger and blow his own brains out.

Dorn pulled him out and dropped onto Joe's chest. *Déjà vu* in reverse. Only it was easy, tragically easy, for Dorn to take the gun out of Joe's hand.

Joe stared at the barrel, pointing in his face. *It's over. I'm dead.*

"Don't shoot him!" Elizabeth screamed. They were all frozen, standing behind Dorn, clearly afraid to do anything now.

Hey idiot! What did I say about giving up too soon? You still have a weapon!

Yes! Joe slid his hand into his pocket as Dorn pointed the gun at his head. He pulled out Francesca's butterfly clip. Some of the guys in school jokingly called those devices "the jaws of life" because they were structured just like a little bear trap. Joe sprung the trap, placed it right over the crotch in Dorn's pants, and let it go.

Dorn screamed. The gun went off just as Dorn dropped it. Joe wondered if he'd been shot. *I'd feel it, wouldn't I?* Instinctively, he'd squished his eyes shut when he heard the gunshot. He opened them to see Dorn staggering and swearing, looking like a wounded bear, falling over the tipped dresser. There was a weird new sound in the background. Like galloping horses. Suddenly the bedroom door blew open and the Men In Black came streaming though like an army of giant ants with their visors and shields and rifles. They boiled into the room, flowing around the walls and then focusing on Dorn, who was just getting the hair clip off his crotch as about ten rifles lunged at his face, all clicking in unison.

Other men were grabbing the kids, pulling them out the door. Someone shouted, "This one's down!" and knelt by Joe. He lifted his visor and showed Joe a friendly, freckled face. "Are you shot?"

"I don't know," Joe said. "He shot at me, but . . ."

"Over here," the freckled man called to some kind of paramedics who had appeared in the doorway.

The room was strangely quiet. There was just the sound of the helicopters in the sky outside and rushing feet going in every direction. And Dorn, sobbing and sobbing, just like Jack Shine had predicted he would.

In twenty-four hours Joe had become a hero.
This meant he, like Francesca, had a private room at Coral
Springs Medical Center. It meant he had a black wind-
breaker that said SPECIAL RESPONSE draped over his
good shoulder. It meant local businesses were offering him,
and his friends, everything from free dry cleaning to college
scholarships. It meant that as soon as Joe was released from
the hospital, which he hoped would be tomorrow, there
would be a million reporters lined up waiting to talk to him.

Francesca had spent most of the afternoon in Joe's
room. There was hardly anything wrong with her, just
some bruises from Dorn slamming her around, but like
Joe, she had to talk to some psychologists before she could
be released. The other kids were getting their counseling
on the outside. She had a chair pulled up now and was
holding Joe's hand and eating cookies from his afternoon
snack tray. They hadn't talked about any of the stuff that
had happened between them. Right now it was enough to
be alive and together. Somehow, Joe wasn't worried. For
one thing, there was no telling how much this whole thing

would change everybody. Maybe Francesca's parents would start caring less about giving Francesca a perfect life and just want her to be happy. Or maybe she'd have the courage to stick up for Joe. He just felt like whatever was supposed to happen, would happen. He realized for the first time since he was a little kid, he believed in . . . well, he wasn't ready to call it God, but he knew something had helped him through that night, and he never wanted to forget that feeling.

Joe and Francesca had watched CNN all day—the same continuous loop of tapes and interviews over and over, so they could almost repeat the dialogue. But they kept wanting to see it. To make sure everything that had happened was real.

They were covering the pizza guy now.

One of the many heroes in this bizarre hostage story is Todd Frankel, a freshman at Florida Atlantic University, earning his tuition by delivering pizzas. Little did he know that his delivery to the now-famous house on Ramblewood Drive could have been his last. . . .

Joe squeezed Francesca's hand as they watched the clip of Todd Frankel, a gangly guy with a scruffy mustache. He was on the third floor. They were supposed to meet him tomorrow. The tape showed him sitting up in his hospital bed, gesturing with his IV arm in big loops.

"I took the call from Joe Anderson. I could hear all the

kids in the background and I knew it was a kids' party and, like, the only thing on my mind was, are these little creeps gonna pay me or stiff me? Huh! So I get to the house and I put her in neutral and I was just reaching around to get the Thermal-Pak—that's always when you feel the most vulnerable—and Dorn jumps in the passenger side and says, 'Take off your clothes.' I wasn't happy. But I did what he said and then he just aims the gun at me and says, 'Sorry.' And I see the gun flash and I'm slammed back into the seat and I say to myself, 'Frankel, you're dead.'"

"You knew it was Dorn?"

"Sure. His face was all over TV that day. They kept saying how he was capping people to get cars and stuff. I worried about it the whole shift, because we're such a target for people like that."

"But even point blank, he didn't seriously wound you?"

"Well, a freakin' bullet went through me! That's serious to me! But he didn't hit anything. He was shaking like a leaf, and he thought my heart was on the right side of my right lung! The bullet went straight through me and into the car. Thank God!"

"So you basically played possum."

"I sure did. Didn't want to get the coup de grace from that maniac. So I just lay there limp, and he went into the Anderson house. I wish, you know, for all those poor kids, I wish I could have grabbed him like James Bond and stopped the whole thing, but I just figured if I tried anything else, I was dead."

"So you drove away and called 911."

"Drove nothing! I didn't want him to hear the car engine. I watched till he was all the way inside, and I called 911 from the driveway, still laying back and keeping my eyes closed, in case he took a look out the window."

"Wow!" Francesca said.

"You know what's weird?" said Joe. "He went to FAU, the same as Dorn. They might have had classes together."

Thanks to Todd's quick thinking, a Special Response Team of the FBI, headquartered in Fort Lauderdale, was able to reach the Anderson house in record time. The response team was coordinated by Special Agent Solomon Page.

Solomon's film clip came on. Joe loved looking at his face.

"Being on the scene early is critical. If we'd come a few minutes later, Dorn might have fled the scene, or harmed the children. Once he knew he was surrounded, he slowed down and got cautious. And literally, kid by kid, we were able to get the hostages out of there."

"Here comes the good part!" Francesca said.

But the youngest hero in this bizarre siege has got to be thirteen-year-old Joseph Anderson."

A still photo came on the screen of Joe's last birthday

party. Then the tape with all the kids except Francesca and Joe, which was shot outside Joe's house.

"All through the whole thing," Steve says. "Joe was large and in charge. Like, he was just so calm! And he kept Dorn talking so he didn't flip out and shoot up the place."

"And he had an escape plan that almost worked!" Elizabeth chimes in. "We kept giving Dorn beer and he was pretty well passed out at one point, and Joe remembered a crawl space in our house that goes to the garage, and he led us through—it was like something in the movies—only Dorn caught us at the last minute."

"But then, Joe didn't give up!" Nathan interrupts. "It was like you could look at Joe through the whole thing and know—he just wasn't gonna give up, and then when things started looking really hopeless—"

"He just jumped him!" Elizabeth again. "I couldn't believe it!"

"A guy with a gun!" Nathan says. "He just grabbed Dorn's hand and knocked the gun away and they started fighting. None of us could even move for a second, and then we sort of unfroze and started helping. . . ."

"We knocked a dresser over on Dorn's legs."

"But the gun was way under the bed, and we couldn't get it."

"And we couldn't get out the door because Dorn was blocking it. . . ."

"And we couldn't get the window open. . . ."

"And then he got loose from under the dresser, and by then

Joe is going for the gun under the bed and he—"
"Put a hair clip on Dorn's crotch! Can we say that?"
"A what? A hair clip?"
"A girls' hair clip. He must have gotten it off the dresser."

"No, he got it from me," Francesca said, smiling at Joe.

"But Dorn is still wrestling him for the gun and it went off!"
"Bang!"

Joe winced at the point where Nathan said bang, even though this had to be the tenth time he'd heard it.

"And the bullet just grazed Joe's shoulder and went into the floor," Elizabeth says.
"And the shot is what made the FBI come in, and they all put rifles on Dorn and took him away. . . ." Nathan takes a huge breath. "And then it was over."

The report picked up with Solomon again.

"All night long, we tried to keep Dorn calm, keep him talking. I recognized right away, Joe was the best hostage, the one who could communicate with Dorn and keep some spark of conscience going. We knew by the fact that Dorn 'allowed' three kids to escape that he really wasn't keen on

hurting the kids. As long as there was no violence, we were gonna keep talking and negotiating all night and into Saturday if we had to. But then at some point, we were talking to him and we could hear a commotion start up. Then the phone went dead. The kids tell me it got smashed by a dresser. We were set up to go in at that point. Then we heard the shot and when you hear a shot, you just go in."

Joe had made a mental note of this. Next hostage situation, grab the gun early on and fire into a wall with everything you've got. Get those guys to come in!

The screen flashed back to the CNN anchor desk.

"Quentin Charles Dorn is now in custody, held without bond, his reign of terror finally at an end. Three young heroes lie in the hospital, all in good condition; Francesca Hart, who suffered contusions in the final scuffle with Dorn, Todd Frankel, the pizza delivery man who lay bleeding in his car, but still made the call that probably saved the children, and, the littlest hero of all, Joe Anderson, the boy with the cool head, who risked everything to save his friends."

"I can't wait to go back to school," Joe said grimly. "Everybody's gonna say, 'Hey! Where's the littlest hero?'"

Francesca squeezed his hand. "Nobody's gonna pick on you after what you've done."

Chandra, one of the nurses, came in. She was Joe's favorite. Everything about her was gentle.

"I thought we were going to turn the TV off and get some rest," she said.

There was nothing on now but the long story on Dorn's background, winding up with his brand-new attorney saying he'd suffered a nervous breakdown and couldn't stand trial. Joe didn't like that segment anyway. He hit the remote and watched Dorn's face shrink and disappear with a little pop.

Chandra said, "Come on, Francesca. Back to your room." She held out her hand.

Joe snuggled down into the jacket Solomon Page had given him. The minute he closed his eyes, pictures flashed in his head—the rifles clicking in Dorn's face, Solomon hugging Joe and throwing the jacket over him, the ambulance ride with Elizabeth and his mom, who kept kissing his hand over and over again. And the beginning—Dorn bursting through the door. Dorn bursting through the door. Dorn bursting through the door . . .

"Hey, pal . . . are you sleepin'?"

Joe opened his eyes, but knew he was still dreaming. Jack Shine was standing at the foot of his hospital bed with a gigantic armload of roses and a shopping bag.

"Hey, Jack!" Joe was used to these apparitions by now.

Shine put down the roses and bag and fingered the towering displays of flowers, cards, and telegrams heaped around Joe's bed. "I heard you were my biggest fan," he said. "And I came to tell you that I'm *your* biggest fan."

Joe sat up a little. This felt an awful lot like reality. For one thing, Shine was talking in this soft, hoarse voice that was nothing like his screaming ring persona. He was dressed in jeans that looked weird, because of the big muscles in his legs. His flowing mane was pulled back in a rubber band. But the really telling thing was his skin. His perfect bronze skin was two shades paler and had stubble and some acne scars.

"You're real!" Joe cried.

Shine laughed. "That's a debatable point, buddy. But if you're asking me if I'm a figment of your painkillers, I'm not. I'm really here. Flew in from Vegas just to talk to you."

"Oh my God!" Tears burned in Joe's eyes. He covered his mouth with both hands, afraid he was going to cry. "How did you find out . . . what made you come here?"

"Your buddies called my boss yesterday. Your friend, Nathan Jericho? But the whole posse got on the phone. Told him you guys were having a Fusion party when Mr. Bad broke in. Said you were a monster fan of The Human Time Bomb. I guess they were trying to get a letter or some tickets or something for you. But hey! I say any kid who has the *cojones* to jump an armed gunman—I want to meet that kid!" As he spoke, Shine was setting out merchandise on Joe's bed: the Jack Shine action figure that yells when you twist its arm, a T-shirt that said YOUR TIME IS UP, a big foam finger that said JACK SHINE IS NUMBER ONE, a pair of real wrestling boots in Joe's size, a watch that said MOMENT OF TRUTH, and the Nintendo game, Rasslin' Rumble.

"This is no big deal," Shine said. "We've got a ton of

this stuff in the warehouse. To be honest, kid, The Human Time Bomb doesn't move his merchandise as well as the younger guys these days. I'm on the bubble, that's for sure."

"On the bubble?"

"Close to retirement. I'm fifty. Forty-five is usually as far as a wrestler gets unless he wants to be a clown or a novelty act. Or the worst thing of all"—he pretended to shudder—"a special guest referee. So when a kid like you still picks a geezer like me for your hero, hey, I like that."

"You'll always be my hero," Joe said. "Whether you're in the bubble or not."

"On the bubble, kid. On the bubble. Anyway, you've done me a favor. My company wants to make an angle out of this. You're a national hero for"—he looked at his watch—"ten more minutes, at least, and my boss wants to exploit that. Here's the deal: Soon as you get medical clearance, we fly you to whatever town our little circus is taping Fusion in, and you do an angle with me on TV. What do you say?"

Joe could feel his heart beating. "Sure! What's an angle?"

"A story line, kid. Like, we'd introduce you from the audience and say you're my special guest, and then a bad wrestler will come out later and pull a gun on me, and you'll rush into the ring and save me. We'll pick some jobber that looks like Dorn. See? It takes no skill whatsoever. I can train you in five minutes. The hardest part will be the six hundred documents and releases your mom will have to sign. But I'll take care of you. We'll be careful not to injure you or any of that stuff. It's bad PR to hurt a kid in the ring."

"I don't even care about that. I'd be on Fusion?"

"Yeah. Prime spot. Top of the nine o'clock hour."

"I must be dreaming!"

Shine patted Joe's good shoulder. "No, kid. You're just waking up from one heck of a nightmare. It's really great what you did for your friends. You're a brave guy."

"Because of you, Mr. Shine."

"Jack!"

"Jack. I always thought about what you would do. That's how I got through it."

Shine turned away suddenly. "Whoops! Got something in my eye. Wow. Both eyes. Hold on." He sniffed, blew his nose, and then turned back to Joe. "Listen. You're a hero, Joe. I just play one on TV. And that's the truth."

"No, you are. Heroes always pick heroes for their heroes," Joe told him.

"Wow. Who said that?"

Joe grinned. "You did."

X X X

Joe's doctor came by after Shine left and told him he had to stay one more night, and if he did okay with the psychologist tomorrow, he could go home. His mother, sister, and friends visited him while he ate dinner. After dinner, he turned the lights down and watched CNN some more, this time with the sound off.

Patrice, another nurse, appeared in his doorway. "Got the energy for one more visitor today? Solomon Page?"

"Absolutely!"

Solomon walked in slowly, smiling his warm smile. He looked at Joe like he was an old army buddy. Suddenly, Joe began to cry.

"What? Is it seeing my face? Does that bring the bad stuff back?" Solomon looked ready to retreat.

Joe couldn't talk. He shook his head no.

"I can go if you . . ."

Joe shook his head vigorously. Patrice, who had been hovering, backed off.

Solomon gave Joe a bunch of Kleenex. "You're probably the only one who hasn't done that yet, anyway. Maybe it's just finally your turn to let go."

Joe nodded and blew his nose. "I'm sorry."

"I don't blame you. You've been holding it in since Friday night. All the other kids cried during their interviews with me. You know, you can't remember stuff like this without . . ." He glanced at the screen, where they were showing Dorn as a teenager, riding a horse.

"Right," Joe said.

"They told me you'll be out tomorrow. You take your time, but soon, I'll need to do a long interview with you, get a detailed statement while everything is clear in your memory. Okay? Because we're going to get this guy, and you're the star witness."

"Count on it," Joe said, looking at the screen again. They were showing the faces of the two people Dorn killed. Solomon looked at the screen, too. His eyes looked sad.

"Do you have kids?" Joe asked.

Solomon looked at Joe. "Yeah. I have two daughters."

"Good. I bet you're a great father."

Solomon cocked his head a little. "Did they tell you your dad is flying in to see you guys at the end of the week?"

"Yeah."

Solomon pulled up a chair and watched the silent images with Joe. "I talked to Dorn today," he said. "It bugs me, this whole story. I look in his face now, and he just looks like an ordinary guy. A kid."

"I know," Joe said. "Sometimes during . . . that night . . . I would forget what he was doing and start to . . . I don't know, think he was a regular guy. Then I'd see the gun and think about what he did and what he might do. . . . It was weird."

On the screen Dorn was being led away from Joe's house in leg irons. Solomon shook his head. "A college kid. Like my daughter! He probably had dreams just like everybody else."

At that moment on the screen, Dorn looked up at the camera and gave a snarling, silent laugh.

The hospital room had gotten dark. Only the flash of the TV illuminated them. The room felt cold to Joe. He pulled Solomon's jacket up around his shoulders. He thought about the ravens. "No," he said finally, "his dreams were different."